No Longer in Uniform

By: Andoni Iapetus

Copyright © 2024 by Andoni Iapetus, LLC

A Note from the Author

My writing journey began as a way to heal—a therapeutic outlet to capture my thoughts and emotions. Translating these feelings onto digital "paper" helped me confront memories and experiences that had been weighing me down, sometimes even disrupting my daily life. Over time, I accumulated a significant collection of what I'll simply call "content." From there, I began to weave ideas and fictional storylines inspired by my life and career. This creative process became transformative, turning burdensome memories into something meaningful and, in a way, cathartic.

Writing provided a safe, productive space to process trauma. When I decided to craft a novel from my "writings," I made a conscious commitment to see it through to publication—a daunting step that both terrified and inspired me. I believed that releasing my concentrated emotions and memories into the larger world could neutralize their power over me—they have. These novels, for me, became the missing ingredient, diluting the bitter concentration of past pain into something palatable, perhaps even nourishing.

As a middle-aged man in search of wisdom once said, *"We are the sum of all our parts—the good, the bad, the ugly, and the beautiful. What matters is what we do with those parts. We have the power to piece them together to create something better, something new, something that can positively impact others. No matter how broken we feel, the journey toward wholeness begins with the choice to reassemble those pieces."*

And as Kurt Vonnegut famously wrote, *"And so it goes."*

I hope my fictional storylines and characters will not only entertain but also inspire others, especially my fellow Veterans, to seek help for their traumas and confront the memories that hold them back. There is strength in facing our past and even greater strength in transforming it into something that lights the way forward.

If you or someone you know is in crisis, please call 988 and get help.

Prologue

The sun began to rise over the treetops to his right on a clear September morning. Normally, this would be a great start to any day; however, Kostas was at a slow crawl in the HOV lanes of I-95 northbound between exit 156 for Dale Blvd and Prince William Parkway. This was nothing new to him. Whether in a vanpool or his own vehicle, he once made this trip religiously to the Center for Combating Weapons of Mass Destruction at Fort Belvoir, Virginia, but that seemed like a lifetime ago now. His mind, now a prisoner to the mocking cadence of WTOP's traffic and weather on the eights, drifted mentally to a similar event of Senator Tim Kaine's experience back in January 2022, when a massive winter system literally froze all traffic. He and a few thousand fellow commuters were stranded with only what they had in their vehicles for over twenty-seven hours. *At least it's September,* he thought, and added out loud to himself, "at least I have water and almonds" with a barely audible chuckle.

Then his mind wandered back to his Richmond office, and the musings that filled his thoughts on this drive—*Why did I agree to this? I hate this drive.* The answer: *To close the deal.* A deal that had been mired in over a year of redline negotiations. He typically didn't get involved in these matters anymore. He had talented people for that now, but this deal was different, due to his experience from a past life and the potential upside for his company, he had been leading this one since day one, and now was wondering if he would ever make it to Tyson's Corner to close the deal. As a news anchor from WTOP mentioned a public service announcement - "kids are back in school" and to "stay alert for buses and children in crosswalks" he came to a complete stop and stared through the driver's side window of his Explorer at the IKEA on his left across the southbound lanes.

As a political candidate's campaign commercial aired on the radio, smearing his opponent's action on immigration, Kostas's world abruptly narrowed. Through the windshield of his dark gray SUV, chaos erupted in front of him, people spilling clumsily from their cars in a frantic exodus southward in panic. His mind shifted gears to the unfolding chaos. He could see panic seizing the air as people abandoned their vehicles in palpable desperation, but from what?

Kostas automatically felt the sympathetic nerve response of the course black hairs on his arms rise, and the feeling of heat on his face and neck as blood began to instinctively shift to his brain, a familiar inner voice spoke to him as it did so many times in the past on the battlefield. It screamed in his head as it did in Iraq and Afghanistan... *"Where's your cover? Where is your egress?"* ... *"You're going to be pinned down"* ... *"MOVE!"*

The automated human response of fight or flight that is programmed in all our DNA kicked in.

He was on autopilot now, without a moment's hesitation, Kostas' training once again commanded his senses and actions. Instinctively, he fell into the ritual of Box Breathing to manage the body's sympathetic response to danger and stress.

In through the nose (four count)- hold (four count)- exhale through the mouth (four count), then repeated the Box sequence three more times as he retrieved his Glock 41 from its secure location within the locked safe located in the center console of the SUV. As he kept his eyes north and exited the vehicle, only then did the sound of gunfire reach his ears. Rapid succession of fire, multiple shooters, he thought to himself.

Intuitively, he crouched low, using the open door as a less-than-perfect ballistic shield while scanning for the threat and then moving to better cover at the rear of the vehicle. The gunfire crescendoed—a cacophony of fully automatic and three-round-burst shots as he witnessed the macabre performance of falling bodies before him.

As the horde of well-dressed commuters came rushing out of their collective BMWs and Mercedes-Benzes toward him, his inner voice urged him again, *"MOVE!"* The southbound lane traffic had now degenerated into a tableau of twisted metal and panic-stricken onlookers. Taking a better position behind a now-abandoned Ford F-350 King Ranch edition that was now skewed against the median barrier, Kostas's dark eyes darted over its hood to assess the scene. Two-point men clad in black tactical gear loomed ahead; one on the shoulder of the northbound lanes, one on the HOV's far shoulder. Their figures, a contrast, almost spectral, against daylight and chaos. They appeared as dark figures clad in all black with tactical vests holding additional magazines for the killing spree, faces obscured by balaclavas and M4 assault rifles that dealt a hand of lethal efficiency in the chaos.

People were falling by the dozens as six additional black-clad assailants took positions slightly to the rear and between the two-point men, forming a sloppy shallow V weaving in and out of the abandoned vehicles or the last resting place of their victims. All were carrying M4 rifles in a rapid dominance formation. The point men drove the prey to the center while the cleanup shooters mowed down the defenseless commuters as they walked in between the tangled mess of vehicles. He removed his coat jacket, then positioned himself in a kneeling shooter's position, right foot behind him and the left knee up, steadying his left elbow as he was drilled so many times before. Kostas had a 4-inch-wide shooting lane just above the F-350's front bumper that was bookended by the truck's grill and the concrete median barrier of the HOV lane.

The attackers' focus was not on Kostas; they hadn't noticed him. Their focus was solely on the innocent lives running away and cutting them down without mercy. The attackers' plan expected no resistance. As the point-man in the HOV lanes trained his weapon on the vulnerable masses, Kostas seized the moment and acted.

As he experienced firsthand multiple deployments and missions, he may not live, but he was sure as hell not going to go down without a fight. Just as his target entered the effective range of his Glock and cleared a painter's pickup truck stacked with a set of large ladders secured to the bed, Kostas had to seize the moment; he unleashed two shots from his .45 toward the nearest assailant. The rounds struck their mark, his upper thighs. The assailant's only exposed area for a shooting solution—the HOV point-man went down.

Three long blasts from a semi-truck's horn then sounded. Simultaneously, the rest of the attackers stopped firing at the end of the third blast, then began an organized retreat to the eastern shoulder of the northbound lanes. The attackers furthest north now acted as point men, and the rest followed in two-by-two formation, the last two covering the retreat from the rear. Two more long blasts sounded, and the retreat continued. Kostas thought that, at least now, he potentially had someone left for questioning by the authorities, and he was alive; that was something.

Rising from his cover, Kostas began to sweep the area with his weapon; left… center… right… Then, in reverse, he made his way to the downed attacker, intending to secure him for the authorities. However, fate had other plans; another solitary horn blast was followed momentarily by a single gunshot.

The wounded man lay still, no more than thirty feet away from Kostas, his secrets carried with him to the grave by his own M4 rifle.

Chapter 1

For Immediate Release

Title: Terror Strikes I-95 and I-64: Coordinated Attacks Leave Two Virginia Locations Reeling

Subhead: Suspected Terrorists Execute Simultaneous Attacks on Major Highways, Escape in White Box Trucks

Date: September 16, 2024

By: Nunzio Vittone for NPR News

WOODBRIDGE, VA and HAMPTON, VA – In a horrifying sequence of events that has stunned the nation, authorities are currently investigating what are being called suspected acts of terrorism after groups of heavily armed individuals carried out coordinated attacks on Interstate 95 and Interstate 64 this morning, causing widespread chaos, bloodshed, and fear.

The first attack unfolded during the morning rush hour on Interstate 95 between exit 156 for Dale Blvd and Prince William Parkway. Suspected terrorists used multiple semi-trucks to block all northbound lanes and the shoulder of I-95, trapping commuters. Eyewitnesses reported that masked gunmen emerged from the trucks and opened fire on the trapped motorists.

Simultaneously, a similar scene was reported at the eastern exit of the eastbound lanes on I-64's Hampton Roads Bridge Tunnel. There, attackers employed identical tactics, using semi-trucks to block traffic before ambushing commuters stranded in the tunnel. The assailants, also dressed in black tactical gear and armed with assault rifles, carried out their attack with coordinated and terrifying precision.

"People were running for their lives. It was like something out of a warzone," recounted an unidentified witness from the I-95 incident, a sentiment echoed by shocked survivors from the I-64 attack.

Approximately thirty minutes after each attack, two white box trucks were found ablaze at separate locations—one near the intersection of Prince William Parkway and Old Bridge Road near I-95, and another close to the Settlers Landing Road exit near I-64. Both vehicles were completely destroyed, significantly complicating efforts to trace the attackers or recover additional evidence.

The motive behind these heinous acts remains unclear, but officials are treating them as acts of terrorism. The FBI, DHS and ATF have joined local authorities in a massive manhunt for the suspects who remain at large after both incidents.

"This is a dark day for our communities," said a spokesperson for the Virginia State Police. "We are working tirelessly to apprehend those responsible for these cowardly attacks and ensure the safety of our citizens."

Both sections of I-95 and I-64 where the incidents occurred remain closed as investigators meticulously comb through the scenes. Commuters are advised to seek alternative routes and remain vigilant.

The attacks have prompted a swift response from state and federal officials. Virginia Governor Marcus Hartley issued a statement condemning the violence and assuring residents that all resources would be directed toward apprehending those responsible.

President LeAntha Adams addressed the nation in a somber tone, expressing her condolences to the victims and their families. She emphasized that such acts of terror will not be tolerated on American soil and promised swift justice for those responsible.

As the investigation unfolds, authorities are calling on anyone with information about either attack or the suspects to come forward. A hotline has been established for tips, and there is a reward for information leading to an arrest.

These tragedies have left deep scars on the nation that will not soon heal. As Virginia and the rest of the country mourn, questions are being raised about how such attacks could have happened simultaneously and what can be done to prevent another occurrence.

This story is developing, and updates will be provided as more information becomes available.

For any tips or information regarding these incidents, please get in touch with the official hotline at 1-888-888-888. Anonymous tips are welcome.

Chapter 2

It was just after one a.m. when Jessica Sparrow's Mercedes GLS 450 left the roundabout on Monument Avenue and pulled into the gated cobblestone driveway of the house nicknamed Olympus, due to its exterior gray stone block construction and white trim that resembled the famous mountain's rock and snow-peaked tops. The driveway continued around the back of Kostas's home in a large horseshoe and then exited back onto Monument Avenue. Access to the complete driveway consisted of four gates, one at the entrance off the road, one that separated the rear of the house from the front, and then a similar layout for the last two that led back out on Monument. All four gates were controlled from a secure app on select cell phones that a close friend developed—Marten Raleigh, also an Air Force veteran who served with Kostas.

Only a small group of individuals had access to the encrypted Bluetooth technology that operated the gates as well as other security features of his home and office. Kostas reached into the back of Jess's Mercedes, where two child booster seats were securely locked down in the SUV's rear, and retrieved his black backpack.

Jess had picked him up from the Amtrak Main Street Station in Richmond's Shockoe Slip area of the city. The previous day's mass casualty event froze all routes in and out of the Northern Virginia corridor of I-95 extending down to Quantico. However, the President issued an emergency order to command all railway activity from New York to Miami, Norfolk to Cleveland in an effort to get survivors either home or somewhere else once they were cleared by authorities. Before Kostas left the I-95 scene, he had grabbed his go-bag of essentials from the back of his Ford Explorer. Thanks to his go-bag, he was able to change from his suit to more suitable traveling clothes before he was escorted from the tragic scene along with the other survivors who were not already transported for medical attention.

"You need me to pick you up in the morning?" asked Jess.

"Not necessary, I'll take the 250 into the office." Referring to the relatively new Ford F-250 in the four-car garage that he occasionally drove, but wasn't practical for everyday use in the Fan District and downtown areas of Richmond.

He then added, "Sleep in and tell Tess sorry for keeping you out all night."

"Good luck parking that beast of a truck downtown. You should think about a more practical vehicle, like mine." She said with a grin.

"With me being born and raised in Dearborn, Michigan, home of Henry Ford, that would be sacrilegious."

"I'll see you at the office at 06:00," she replied with a grin.

Kostas was thankful to have Jess as a part of his company, Meraki Government Solutions Incorporated. In her mid-forties, Jessica Sparrow was nearly as tall as Kostas with a slim athletic build that was all toned muscle from the active lifestyle she led with her wife and kids not to mention her intense CrossFit routine. She had slightly predatory features in the genetic make up of her face, a stark contrast to her friendly bright blue eyes. The former Army Intel officer first met Kostas after her separation from active duty service in the US Army as a linguist and cryptologist. At that time, she was a civilian in the Air Force's Intel community. She respected his no-nonsense pragmatic ways in briefings, underscoring mission success over all else. The fact that politics never played into the scenario for Kostas admittedly didn't always go over well with superiors, however his contemporaries and peers respected him for it.

With a nostalgic appreciation for the "I'll do what I want grin" she displayed, Kostas gave her a quick salute and walked into the back door of his house.

Jess was incredibly capable of being a chief operating officer with any Fortune 500 company, and Kostas knew that. Years prior, he wisely seized the opportunity and made a deal with Jess to leave her safe and predictable civil service career and come to his then-startup company. The deal consisted of using her skills and capabilities to support him directly in the corporation, versus what it would take to support an entire workforce and corporate structure.

She was never to be mistaken for a personal assistant or admin; she was the chief operating officer of Kostas's business life and, on rare occasions, his personal life. She was good at recognizing his subtle signs of stress and post-traumatic stress disorder when almost no one else could. As a combat veteran herself, she kept an eye out for his mental well-being as many military veterans do for each other when they see signs of crisis looming.

In exchange for keeping him on schedule and out of trouble, he would facilitate the life she desired from a career perspective; she and Tess would raise a family together. So far, she has raised no complaints about the deal they made, only occasional criticisms of his sometimes-unorthodox actions as a caring sister would.

He paid her as a Fortune 500 C-level executive. She was worth every penny.

"Try not to wake Tess or the kids when you get home," he said jokingly as he closed the car door.

Chapter 3

The vibrating alarm began to pulse rhythmically from his watch at 4:00 a.m. He went down to the basement, swam only half of his normal three thousand meters then showered and dressed for the office.

As the garage door opened, he disarmed the security features within and climbed into the Ford F-250, then headed down Monument Avenue east, then north on Arthur Ashe Boulevard to hit the on-ramp from Robinhood to I-64 East headed downtown.

Kostas Papadopoulos, known during his Air Force days as Alpha, short for Alphabet. A name that was given to him in basic training by the military training instructors due to the string of letters that composed his family's name. He stood with his cup of morning coffee framed by the broad floor-to-ceiling southern-facing window of his Richmond, Virginia, office that overlooked the James River. To his right, the skyline stretched across the western window of his corner office on yet another clear, bright, early autumn morning, similar to yesterday's start of the day that quickly turned tragic on the interstates.

Once a sharp-witted Major in the USAF, known for his pragmatic approach to leadership and operations, as well as an acumen for national security and counterterrorism operations. Now, he deployed those experiences and expertise by performing on a series of contracts with the federal government and Department of Defense as well as allied countries of the United States with the company he founded.

His Greek American ancestry had bequeathed him a natural steadfast resolve and a stereotypical Mediterranean vindictiveness for those who harmed the ones he cared about or his country. An instinctual and inherited legacy that thrummed in his veins as he faced down each new challenge throughout his life. With every sip of the dark Blanchard's coffee that fueled his mornings, Kostas allowed himself a private momentary swell of emotion.

He had soared beyond the rigid structure of the Air Force and the chaos of combat, yet the battle for peace was an enduring campaign both for his own mind and the nation and its Allies. He gazed out across the river and pondered the illusion of safety and peace here in the United States, knowing that they were a luxury that required constant vigilance and action to maintain.

With a sad, self-deprecating grin reflecting back at him from the window, Kostas whispered… You can't handle the truth. A dark but very real reality portrayed by Jack Nicholson in the movie A Few Good Men, highlighting the average citizen's enjoyment of freedom, without the knowledge or burden of what it takes to maintain it. Yesterday's failure of intelligence was too close; he wanted answers and not just the who, but why and how they knew.

As the sun continued to rise, Kostas closed the office curtains. Using a digital smart board in his office, he began to document and analyze the events from yesterday on I-95, recalling every detail from the news reporter's voice on the radio, to the view of the IKEA to his left, and then the chaos that ensued. He had given his statement first to the State Police and then again to an investigator with Homeland Security. His unemotional, almost robotic responses were kept concise and based on observed facts and not speculation.

How did they know? he asked himself again in worried confusion.

Once more, Kostas Papadopoulos found himself on the pitch of the match between terrorism and counterterrorism, where shadows loom with hidden dangers and threats lurk around every turn, now on home soil. Driven by a deep sense of duty and bewilderment, he exhaled with gritted teeth… How did they know?

"Good morning, Sir," came Jess's voice from his office doorway, retrieving him from his thoughts. "There's a call for you. It's General Morris."

"Thank you Jess," he replied.

"He doesn't sound happy, not that he ever does," she replied with a respectful grimace.

Nodding with a scoff, he replied, "You are right about that, Jess."

He punched the green button on the conference table's phone. "WHERE THE HELL ARE YOU?" came the slightly southern and agitated drawl from the speakerphone.

It was good to hear Wade's voice after the events of the last twenty-four hours, even if it was in the form of a bark.

"Well, General," keeping formalities on the chance that others were listening on the line, "you called me, so where do you think I am?" Kostas replied with an unintentional but instinctual grin as they played this game on the phone many times before.

"You know I am no longer in uniform, right?"

"Cut the shit, Alpha! Why the hell didn't you stay up north?"

"It's not my job to stay, Wade," he replied, dropping all formalities and the grin.

" I need you up here, now! And before you say another word... I have an A&AS contract signed right now for MGSI."

Referring to the Department of Defense's terminology of Advisory and Assistance Services contracts that are used for specific circumstances that necessitate external expertise that is not readily available within the DoD itself. Kostas's company, Meraki Government Solutions Inc., or MGSI, already had several of these contracts awarded to them over the past several years.

"I can't have you running around as a CIV without you being under contract." He added, using a shortened version of civilian to get his point across.

Kostas wanted to reply with a sharp protest. He was barely on the other side of twenty-four hours since the attack yesterday, and he was right in the middle of the carnage. He wanted to say, "I already told the investigators on scene all that I knew," but he understood that there was more to Wade's request than what happened yesterday on the interstates. It was about the Mock Incident Scenario Program, or MISP, that he participated in while with the 609th Air Operations Group.

Now with a tone of resigned understanding, Kostas asked, "Belvoir?"

"No, it's still a shit show there... FBI, NSA, DHS, congressional aides, State Police, you name it they might was well invite the fucking Cub Scouts! Every one of them is all outrage, finger pointing and no action," he paused, "The Dulles Room."

Referring to a secure, little-known conference room located at Dulles Airport that was primarily utilized when foreign Government representatives wanted to meet face-to-face with their US counterparts, but our government did not want them to leave the airport grounds and wander around the US unescorted.

"Get over to the Sandston Army Aviation Unit at Richmond International, a Black Hawk is being readied now," said Wade.

"A flight?" Kostas asked as he noticed his palms starting to sweat.

"I know it's not ideal for you but put on your big boy pants and get airborne damn it. I don't have time for you to drive around the incident scene to get here." Wade barked.

"Do I need to pack a bag?" asked Kostas with a slight hint of sarcasm as a nervous reaction to Wade's comment about the helicopter. *God, I hate flying*, he thought.

"You know this would be a whole lot simpler if you WERE still in uniform; get on the GOD DAMN helicopter Alpha." was the only reply, then silence. Wade hung up.

As Kostas exited his office in a purpose-driven stride, from her office door, Jess intuitively handed him a backpack, anticipating short-notice travel given the circumstances of the last twenty-four hours and the call from General Morris. The pack, almost identical to the one he retrieved from the back of his Explorer at the I-95 scene, had a change of clothes fit for traveling as well as other nice-to-haves.

The bag also had a distinctive red colored handle at the top that signified that it also contained loaded weapons. Specifically, a Glock 41 and a smaller compact Glock 30 with two different holsters, one a black leather shoulder rig with a two-magazine pouch. The second, an inside-the-waistband holster, could interchangeably fit both handgun models.

The Glock that he retrieved from his SUV during the attack yesterday was placed into evidence by law enforcement, a standard procedure. Jess would coordinate its retrieval once the investigation authorized it. Also contained in the backpack were four spare magazines fully loaded, one additional mag already in the mag-well of each weapon. For safety purposes, there was no round racked to the chamber, a stark difference from Kostas's normal practice of always having the weapon chambered and ready to fire with the 230 grain Federal Hydra-Shok .45 ACP jacketed hollow point or JHP round.

Chapter 4

Kostas's truck turned off Beulah Rd onto Falcon Drive and swerved at a high rate of speed through the concrete barrier serpentine just before the front access gate. Due to the nature of the flight, Wade had told him the Black Hawk would be ready on the alert ramp of the old Air Guard side of the airport and not off the Army Guard's Portugee Road ramp. As he continued through the security serpentine, the State-employed gate guard ran from the gatehouse and stopped in front of his truck at the ID checkpoint.

"What the hell are you doing? You're speeding, it's clearly posted at 15 mph!" barked the gate guard through the truck's window.

Kostas knew the guy was just doing his job; however, he was not in the mood.

"How fast was I going?" he asked.

The guard started to stammer, "You were speee…"

"You don't know how fast, do you?" He interrupted with an authoritative voice. "I suggest before you accuse someone of an offense, you have some data to back it up," replied Kostas.

The guard made a show of pulling a ticket book from his belt and took a pen out of his shirt pocket. "Give me your driver's license," the guard said confidently.

Kostas simply replied, "No," and then he added, "I don't think you want to start that ticket. You will spend more time undoing it and explaining your actions than issuing it." He said with a dead-eyed stare in the guard's reflective sunglasses.

As the guard started to stammer, "Thaatttt's how you want to plllaaay this, I …"

Kostas interrupted him again as his eyes turned from the guard to the front of the truck, "My escort is here, that will be all."

Bewildered by the response and unsure of anything at this point, the guard turned around to see the approaching Flag Officer car, noted by the one-star on the front license plate as well the vehicle's hood that was decorated with a miniature American flag on one corner and the Air Force flag on the opposite.

"That will be all." Kostas reiterated, then put the truck into drive. Leaving the gate guard thoroughly confused, frustrated and alone at the checkpoint.

He continued to follow the escort vehicle to the backside of the Flight Operations building. Jess would later arrange for the truck to be picked up. Kostas exited the truck with his backpack and was greeted by a full bird colonel in a flight suit whom he did not know. "Mr. Papadopoulos, this way Sir." Said the full bird.

As he entered the Ops building, he was handed a flight suit with no insignia or markings, but he noticed it was his size. "No thanks, too short of a trip" he said and handed it back to the Staff Sargent. The Colonel nodded. "I only need a headset and comms" he said.

Referring to the dual-purpose hearing protection and communication device used on helicopters. The Colonel nodded to the Staff Sargent again.

Kostas checked the condition and the fit of the headset then nodded to the Colonel, then replied "Ready."

As the final flight safety checks were being performed, Kostas swapped his now daily uniform of custom-tailored suits from Franco's for the more practical attire that was contained in the pack. His suits and sport coats were all custom fit to soften the necessary lines of his concealed weapons that he carried when needed. Dark gray KUHL slacks, a black short-sleeved collared golf-style shirt marked with MGSI's insignia, and opting to keep his signature black Doc Marten 1460's boots on as the Black Hawk's rotors started to spin. He began his ritual of preflight breathing, inhale, hold, exhale, hold, and repeat. The entire transition from his office to IAD unfolded in just a little over two hours.

Momentarily after touchdown, he received a thumbs up from the crew chief. He navigated his way beneath the helicopter's spinning rotors, the prop wash buffeting him as he exited onto the ramp. His eyes quickly found Wade, emerging from a black Chevrolet SUV.

"What took you so long?" Wade's voice was rough, almost accusatory.

"Next time, have the Air Guard pick me up instead of the Army Guard," Kostas shot back, wiping his sweaty palms on his pant legs.

A hint of warmth softened Wade's features. "Good to see you, Alpha."

"Same," Kostas responded.

The short drive was steeped in silence, punctuated only by the hum of the SUV's engine as the Army General's aide steered them toward a distant hangar, far removed from the airport's bustling concourses. Upon arrival, they were met by another aide, who dashed from the hangar's partially open door, a tablet and phone clutched in his hands.

As the driver held the door for Wade, the second aide mirrored the gesture for Kostas. "Welcome to Dulles, Sir," he shouted over the roar of the airport's jet noise and the Blackhawk's rotors. Kostas offered no response, maintaining his stoic demeanor as the aide gestured for him to follow in the General's wake.

Inside the dimly lit, seemingly empty hangar, only a small fraction of the lighting was illuminated for a balance of safety and concealment precautions. Their small group moved swiftly toward the back where two young female Marines stood at attention, their M4 rifles a silent testament to their vigilance of their assigned task. After Wade acknowledged them with a curt "as you were," one extended an ID pack and lanyard to Kostas, which he donned. The ID bore his image from his last Common Access Card or CAC while still in the Air Force as a Major, a second card had a bold red number signifying top-tier security clearance and his authority to be present in highly classified environments.

At the far end of the hangar, in a small conference room, a solitary monitor screen perched on a movable stand faced the end of a long conference table. Four individuals were seated at the table, their attention fixed on the approaching men. As Wade entered, all present, including those in civilian clothes, stood at attention in a unified motion of respect.

Kostas had an intimidating physical presence in almost any room. At the age of fifty-one, he still had the physique of a V-shaped torso comprised of broad shoulders and an agile waist, albeit showing signs of age and wear. The shape and stature of his body were credited to genetics, morning swims of three thousand meters in his basement's Olympic-sized pool, and his diet.

He stood at five-eleven, shorter than both his father and brother, but there was no mistaking their inherited family build and facial features. He could no longer run or perform high-impact activities due to several old injuries that were continuing to age with him. Nonetheless, he had a significant physical presence with a stoic demeanor and piercing eyes that commanded attention, if not respect. When in his presence, you were either drawn to him or were intimidated by him instinctively, and sometimes both. If his physical presence didn't command the room, when he spoke, his natural, deep, and projecting voice did.

"As you were," replied Wade as he entered and stood behind the chair at the head of the table, and everyone except for Kostas took their seats.

As the representatives from different military and federal agencies sat, Wade took his seat at the head of the table, Kostas stood two paces behind Wade's left shoulder, signifying to everyone in the room that he reported directly to General Morris, and he was there at the General's command.

"Everyone, this is Kostas Papadopoulos, I have brought him in on this Joint Task Force due to his unique background and perspective that he can bring to this shit show, he is cleared at the appropriate level and has full access to all information regarding the I-95 and I-64 attacks."

"Now, give me the updates." Wade barked at the individuals at the table.

The first to speak out of ambition or the simple fact that he was too nervous to endure the silence was a pudgy middle-aged man wearing what looked to be a gray suit from a Macy's department store that he might have slept in. "Sir," he stammered, "We have yet to link this event to any known terrorist factions or—" Wade cut him off.

"I said updates, NOT a recap!" he yelled.

The chubby gray suit shrank back into his chair and did his best to melt away from Wade's ire.

Next, with a small cough she cleared her throat giving herself time to reconsider speaking or just formulating her thoughts. She was an attractive woman with straight dark red hair that was clipped into an FBI regulation, seemingly tall with an athletic build, judging by her stature as she sat at the table with her back as straight as possible. She wore the FED's typical black blazer and white blouse, and maybe matching black pants or skirt, Kostas couldn't tell from his angle behind Wade.

She stood looking down at her notes on her laptop, cleared her throat once more, then in a confident tone began, "General Morris, we have identified the deceased attacker as Geraldo Rizzarrero, US Marine Corps, dishonorable discharge October 2006 for human trafficking. The trafficking involved mostly children of TCNs in the Middle East."

Referring to Third Country Nationals, a status that allows individuals who are citizens of one country to live and work within another. The United States Department of Defense, at times, will contract with companies that hire TCNs to work in low-level service positions such as janitorial services on remote or foreign military bases around the world, particularly in the Middle East. At times, the need for work and pay overrides the potential risks of having fewer legal rights and protections compared to citizens for these desperate individuals. These distressed job seekers frequently become prey for profits for unscrupulous contractors who control their fates by creating a litany of dependencies that limit their bargaining power for basic rights, pay, and freedom, making them more vulnerable to exploitation.

She continued, "…Born September 9th, 1982, in Glendale, California. Married to a Colleen McMoore of Copperas Cove, Texas, kept her maiden name, never took the name Rizzarreo. Currently residing in a rural area of southeast Michigan. She has a long arrest record for fraud, petty theft, and domestic violence. Lately, she has been picked up by the intel community's monitoring of social media chatter. She seems to have an affinity for rhetoric on anti-government sites, most recently this morning. Rizzarreo's body had no personal effects nor ID; he was positively identified by his fingerprints from his enlistment into the Corps. Additionally, his ID was confirmed by his tattoos, which were recorded previously in his military records. No body armor. The tactical vest was manufactured by ZeroPen Tactical in Elizabeth City, North Carolina. We are checking orders and lot numbers now. ZeroPen is fully cooperating. The M4's lower receiver had no manufacturer markings; it was definitely illegally manufactured, but expertly built. All the other components had their serial numbers removed, either by melting or grinding.

One more thing on Rizzarreo, his boots were…."

"Issued," Kostas interrupted with a deep and commanding voice, meaning issued by the US military.

The now confirmed tall female Agent stood and immediately turned to Kostas, then with a bit of an incredulous and accusatory tone asked, "How did you know that?"

Now it was Wade's turn to interrupt. "Agent Hogan, Papadopoulos here is I-95 witness number N224 in the redacted incident report."

"The operator and shooter bystander?" Hogan asked incredulously.

"The same," Wade replied with a curt nod.

Kostas started, "I'm not an Oper…" but Wade cut him off with a small backward glance over his shoulder.

"General, this is…" Hogan began hotly and was also cut off by Wade, this time with his words.

"Agent Hogan, this is an active Joint Task Force investigation into a suspected terrorist attack under a dual-status command structure. In case you missed the memo, President Adams, in her infinite wisdom issued an Executive Order, in accordance with the Stafford Act;" Which established framework for the DoD to lead investigations and the defense of the Nation in certain matters. He continued, "that I happen to be in charge of, NOT the FBI Agent Hogan. Again, my office is in charge of this investigation with assistance from the FBI and other agencies around this table. Am I understood?" barked Wade.

Visibly irritated with a reddened face that was turning a deeper shade of crimson moment by moment, almost achieving the same shade of her hair, Hogan replied, "yes, sir." And let her eyes fall to the keyboard in front of her on the table, but she remained standing.

Wade began with a loud but sarcastic tone, "Now that is taken care of, since you couldn't wait to interject Alpha, please by all fucking means continue."

Kostas stepped from behind the General and stood at the whiteboard on his left. Hogan sat but never took her eyes off Kostas.

"As you began to point out, Agent Hogan, the boots were issued, maybe not bucket issued,"

Referring to Marine Corps boot camp issuing of equipment and uniforms, "but definitely US Marine Corps regulation."

He continued… "Boots to some military members are like a favorite pet or lucky talisman; they don't part with them lightly. They wear their boots to the grocery store in and out of uniform; they wear them to do yardwork around the house. Some even wear them to blue-collar jobs after leaving the military. It could be out of necessity for good quality boots or just pride. I've seen enough issued boots in my days to recognize them, regardless of the individual issuing military branch."

Hogan's eyes looked down at Kostas's boots, but he said nothing and continued to listen: "Rizzarreo's were well worn and with more than just blood, oil, or dirt on them. The left boot had a dog tag laced up in it. I could see that it was there; I just couldn't read it without cutting the laces free." He paused, looking directly at Agent Hogan: "Did your forensics team check that out? They probably could have identified him hours earlier."

Hogan just glared at him with fury in her eyes that matched her dark red hair.

He continued, "I guess not. As his Tac-Gear and rifle appeared to be new with no wear and tear visible, a stark contrast to his boots. Add the well-coordinated attack that must have been well planned and well-practiced to operationally succeed at two locations simultaneously. Also, from a quick observation of the spent brass at the scene while I was waiting for the response from LEO."

Referring to Law Enforcement Officers.

"It occurred to me that it was likely the group of attackers was well funded, but not Al-Qaeda circa 2001 well funded, nonetheless, they were well funded. Rizzarreo was wearing new tactical gear, and the M4 was custom-made, not purchased or issued by a military organization or LEO. Additionally, the spent brass was a mixture of .556 and .223 calibers with several different manufacturer head stamps. They were spot buying ammo on the US consumer market, either online or at big-box sporting goods stores. All the headstamps that I came across were from commercial manufacturers. It was obvious that they were not purchasing by lot or full production, as most military organizations and governments do around the world."

Hogan shot back, even more visibly agitated, "So, you tampered with evidence at a scene of a crime?"

"No, as I said, just observed." Kostas calmly but deliberately replied, not breaking eye contact with her.

The room felt uncomfortable for the rest of the individuals sitting around the table in the resulting silence, a standoff of wills and egos between the two.

Wade had had enough; he slammed his palm against the top of the solid wood conference table, startling everyone except for Hogan and Kostas, who continued to stare at each other. Then he said, "Piss on each other's legs on your own time… Carl, where are we on the second scene and getaway vehicles? That was Homeland Security's action item." Wade interjected, de-escalating the standoff.

As another cheap gray suit stood, Kostas's eyes swiveled to the right, away from Hogan. His eyes now engaged the eyes of a tall and slender mid-forties man. "Sir," Carl began, "forensics is still finalizing the preliminary report for both I-95 and I-64 scenes. Drone shots for both locations are on the monitor; here are their corresponding satellite images. These are the best that we could get, given no notice of attack. Mr. Papadopoulos is correct, both scenes had a mix of .556 and .223 casings, none of the headstamps trace back to US or NATO official procurements. Commercial building security cameras and traffic cams are still being analyzed. No reported pings so far from VDOT on any speed cams, only traffic cams after the attacks near their respective scenes during the van's egresses."

"Anything additional on the lane blocking trucks from either scene?" Wade asked.

"Nothing yet, Sir. We estimate the plates were stolen. Regarding the getaway vans, fires destroyed all other identifying markers and contents; accelerants were used. We are trying to recover serial numbers off the engine blocks and other parts that have not been fully destroyed, as well as identify the type of accelerant," Carl replied.

"So, we know nothing," Wade grunted.

Kostas interjected, "General Morris," showing the respect that Wade's rank demanded in front of this group. "Are we cleared to discuss…" Once again, Wade cut him off before he could finish.

"Ladies and gentlemen," Wade began. "All of you are familiar with the Air Force's 609th Air Operations Center and its mission out of Al Udeid Air Base, Qatar, in recent years. What you may or may not know is that its subcomponent, the 609 Air Operations Group, was headquartered out of Shaw Air Force Base back in the '90s. Papadopoulos here was part of that unit of worldwide specialty advisers. He was detailed from the 609th to DTRA's Washington Technical Support Group shortly after DTRA was formed."

"Verum-I Perlustro Verum-I Reperrlo?" asked Hogan, seeming a little impressed.

"Yes, I search the truth; I find the truth," Wade replied with a wisp of nostalgia. Your Latin is good, as is your knowledge of DTRA. That is where Papadopoulos and I, as a young Major, first worked together. Anyway, we operated within the DTRA's Washington Technical Support Group, in Program Paratiro. We were charged with developing Mock Incident Scenario Programs, or MISPs."

"To observe?" Hogan interrupted again, referring to Program Paratiro.

"Your Greek is also good," said Wade, "yes, sort of a perverted think tank for lack of a better phrase. We would create mock scenarios to observe and learn from in hopes of preventing or responding better to the next OK City or Khobar Towers bombings. It was a joint operation between the DoD and other three-letter agencies. Our friend here, known back then as Alpha, led a scenario where all traffic lanes on I-95 would be blocked using multiple vehicles, then a small tactical strike group would massacre trapped commuters."

"Jesus Christ." Carl mumbled under his breath as all the color in his face drained to presumably his DSW purchased black loafers.

"Yes, just that Carl and then some," Wade replied, "Seems like someone took that peach of an idea and decided they could scale it a bit."

"Did I miss anything, Kostas?" Wade asked.

"From a high level brief, no Sir," Kostas replied. "I would only add that the original scenario for the I-95 study was for a foreign terror group attack on US soil, not domestic terrorists like Oklahoma City."

"Why the distinction?" Carl asked.

With a shrug of his shoulders, Wade replied, "That was one of the assumptions made to scope out the scenario. As most projects within a program start out, it was given a problem statement: How could a foreign terror organization inflict a massive amount of death and fear in the Capital Region and on the American People? Many of us came up with the same ol' same ol'… dirty bomb in a trunk of a car detonated remotely while parked on a street in DC, subway mass casualty events, or an airliner hijacking. Kostas came up with the mass shooting scenario involving the interstate system. Low-tech, high casualty-rate, little to no resistance, the attackers could escape and live to fight another day, unlike 911."

"There is no way this is a coincidence; someone just came up with that same idea?" Said the man only known as Jim from DIA or Defense Intelligence Agency.

"Not likely." replied Kostas, then added, "That is the most concerning thing to me, there were several plausible MISPs that were developed during the program."

Jim asked, "Besides you two, who else was on that project or had access to the whole program?"

Wade spoke up again, "All the names, official files and their last known whereabouts are in a JWICS communication,"

Referring to DIA's Joint Worldwide Intelligence Communications System, "all of you can access the info as well as other projects within the MISPs back at your respective SCIFs." Or Sensitive Compartmented Information Facility, locations where the intel community can safely access highly classified information. Wade continued, "Agent Hogan, I assume you will be taking the lead on tracking our ex-compadres in arms from Program Paratiro?"

"That is correct General, I'll get FBI assets on it immediately." Hogan replied, then with a snort of contempt added, "At least I know where he was at during the attack." Adding a jerk of her head toward Kostas.

"Enough." was all Wade said.

"We all have our assignments listed either here or in the secure comms, are there any questions?" Wade asked. "No? Then get out of here and bring me back their fucking heads! We will meet as needed via secure comms and in person again later this week for more updates, and I better have updates damn it!"

Wade rose from the table, and everyone came back to attention, including Kostas. "As you were," Wade ended the meeting before moving to the hangar to speak with his aide.

As everyone else gathered their laptops and files, Kostas went to follow Wade out the door, but Agent Hogan cut him off before he could get out. "Fancy boots for an operator," she said as her eyes went from his Doc Martins and slowly back up again to meet his eyes.

He realized it was more a flirtation than an insult. "Who said I was an operator?" he replied dryly.

With a small tilt of her head and a squint of her eyes, she asked, "Well, aren't you?"

"More of an analyst," he replied.

"Really? A Tom Clancy reference to Jack Ryan?" she scoffed again, then replied, "I don't believe that for a minute. Maybe a contracted merc." She was using the slang term for mercenaries.

"Believe what you will, as you said; I search the truth; I find the truth." With that, he walked past her to meet Wade back at the SUV.

Once Kostas and Wade were both in the SUV, he asked, "What's with her?"

"Are you asking about the professional sparring between you two?" Wade said with a grin. It's your outgoing personality." He added in a teasing tone while shaking his head back and forth, then continued, "It's the same situation that I have observed with you for over twenty years… women want you; men want to be you."

"Neither would if they really knew me."

Wade, laughing now, added, "I whole heartily agree, my friend, I whole heartily agree." Then he trailed off. After a long pause, Wade looked back at Kostas, then added, "You know, this would be a lot easier if you were still in uniform."

Kostas looked at him with his stoic expression then said, "Not going to happen Wade."

After another few moments of silence passed in the vehicle, Wade asked, "When was the last time you spoke with Marika?"

Kostas stared out the window and replied, "Too long."

Chapter 5

Wade and Kostas returned to Ft. Belvoir on the same Black Hawk that flew Kostas to Dulles, a brief trip.

"What's your next move?" Wade asked Kostas from the LZ.

"The wife," Kostas said as he wiped his palms on his pants again, referring to Rizzarreo's widow.

"What do you need?" replied Wade.

"Am I authorized to carry a sidearm?" Kostas asked.

"Yes, it's part of the scope of the contract, and an encrypted electronic copy is in your company email. Jess provided the bilateral signature agreeing to the terms with the Army's contracting officer. She's the one who asked for the scope to be increased to carry a firearm and authorize lethal force in performance of the contract. She's good."

"The best and forget it. You can't bring her back into the fold, you'll never be able to pry her away from me, let alone her wife and kids." Kostas replied.

"It was worth a shot." Wade quipped back with a small smile.

"So, who do you want to take with you to interview the wife?" asked Wade.

"No one," he replied.

"Thought you would say that. Get the rest of your cred-pack and for god's sake, update that picture, you look like you're still in high school. I will have a driver for you, the car will be waiting here in front of the building for you by the time you're done. Report back by 19:00," Wade replied.

"WILCO," Kostas replied as they parted ways in the security lobby of the seven-story building. Kostas had a few tasks to take care of.

"And no god damn first class flights, you're on a government contract now." Wade barked over his shoulder as they parted.

"Jess will square it up before we invoice you,, General, " he replied loudly and walked to the security lockers before the x-ray machines and facial recognition scans.

Chapter 6

After obtaining his updated credentials, he made his way back through security and then picked up his backpack from the locker before exiting the building. As promised, a GSA-issued, white four-door sedan was waiting. The driver, a young corporal, made his way to Fort Belvoir's Legal Office Building after receiving Kostas's instructions. As Kostas stepped out of the car, the young soldier asked, "Sir, shall I go with you?"

"No. Return to General Morris's office and request four copies of my contract in an appropriately marked classified folder, suitable for transport. Meet me back here in an hour and wait for me." Then he closed the car door.

He entered the building, then flashed his credentials for the security team, and one of the guards motioned to the lockers for him to place his backpack. After clearing security, he made his way to the third floor. He entered room 325 and walked up to the receptionist. "Here to see Lieutenant Colonel Ester Yeager."

A young female corporal looked at him from behind her monitor, puzzled. "Colonel Yeager?" she asked.

"Yes, Ester Yeager, please," Kostas said with a direct, unmovable conviction.

The young corporal closed the sliding glass window at the desk and scurried away into the back.

"Ma'am, there is a gentleman here looking for you."

"Did I miss an appointment?" asked the colonel worriedly from behind her desk, pulling up her Outlook calendar.

"No, ma'am." The response came back.

"Please assist the gentleman with making an appointment, Sandra."

"Yes, ma'am… eh, ma'am, does the name Ester mean anything? He asked for Lieutenant Colonel Ester Yeager," the corporal added.

Yeager immediately flushed red, instantly intimidating the young corporal. The young soldier thought she had made some unrecoverable error. "Ma'am, I ammm Sorr…" she tried to spit out.

"It's okay, Sandra. You didn't do anything wrong. I will be out there in a minute. Please tell him to wait in the lobby."

"Yes, ma'am," replied the young corporal, then left.

As Colonel Marika Yeager rose from her desk, she straightened her Air Force blues, the uniform of the day, then adjusted her gig-line, matching her uniform blouse button row to the edge of her belt buckle.

She said to herself, "God dammit Kostas" with both a hint of joy and frustration simultaneously. She would never admit it to him, but she did smile after the corporal exited the doorway.

Colonel Marika Yeager's maiden name was Mavros, a popular Greek family name. Now, several years divorced from her abusive husband.

She met Kostas while stationed at Shaw AFB, South Carolina, back when he was still a captain. Back then, Yeager, a bright young "butter-bar" lieutenant at the time, was barely a year out of Officer Training School. Her first introduction to Kostas Papadopoulos was less than an ideal fairytale introduction; at that time, he was nothing more than a file on her desk that was pending disciplinary action proceedings.

Less than a year later, their careers intersected again, and a friendship and mutual admiration for each other developed. After that, Kostas would make a habit of teasing her about her first name, Marika. To him and many Greek Americans, it was the equivalent of the name Ester, an old name that hardly anyone named their daughters in the US, let alone in Greece.

Just as Hollywood has repeatedly depicted in movies, everyone in a Greek family is named after an Orthodox saint, like Nickolas, and a plethora of derivatives of Nickolas, like Nick, Niko, Nikki, Nicole, Nicoletta, and so on, are common. The same goes with Mary, Christ's mother; Mary, Maria, Marina, Melina, Marina, and Marika, to name a few. The last, Marika, was only known to little old Greek yiayas or grandmothers as the name skipped a generation or two for some unknown reason.

Kostas found a quirky but funny vulnerability in Marika to exploit in jest and called her Ester at times just to tease her, knowing that it got under her skin. The first time he called her Ester in jest, she instantly shot back hotly with a "that's not funny!", immediately identifying the reference and her irritation with it. It has stuck ever since.

With an air of command, Yeager stepped out from a solid windowless door into the waiting area. "Really, Kostas, I mean really?" she scolded. Sandra tried to hide her smile behind the reception desk's monitor and quickly excused herself to some unknown destination.

"Good to see you, Marika," Kostas said through a large, toothy smile.

"Get back here before you make a spectacle of both of us" she commanded and held the door open.

"Yes, ma'am," he quipped.

"Second door on the right," she ordered. Once inside a small conference room, she closed the door and said, "What the hell, Kostas?"

"Got 'cha," he smiled again.

Yeager began to laugh, "Damn you!" and continued the laugh.

"Are you here on Belvoir for what I think you are?" she asked.

"How's the joint pilot program with the Air Force and the Army's Legal Office going?" was his only reply.

Letting out a deep breath, she said, "Fine," conceding that an answer was not forthcoming. She knew that his past and present life revolved around national security, and she had served in the military's legal system as long as she had. Marika knew not to ask too many questions, even if she really wanted the answers from him.

"I'm only here for a few hours," he said.

"Wade?" she asked.

He gave a single nod and then added, "I wanted to see you; it's been too long."

"Can't you ever stop by when you can be around for more than a few hours?" she retorted.

He smiled as he said, "You can always come down to Richmond."

"Kostas…" She began.

He interrupted, "Hey, how about in a few weeks we go to the lake, take a week off together?"

She smiled and laughed, "Can you pull yourself away from MGSI that long?"

"I know the owner; he's Greek. I'll tell him I met a nice Greek girl… he'll understand." Kostas replied with a chiclet grin.

She laughed that genuine laugh that Kostas knew only she had. That laugh always made Kostas feel warm, happy, and safe. She then added, "By the way, my parents are still wondering what happened to that nice Greek boy I used to date."

"Used to date?" he asked, somewhat shocked.

"Well, what would you call it?" she shot back.

"Fair," he conceded.

"A few weeks and it's a date? Pack your bikini." He continued with a hopeful look on his face.

"Now you're really pissing me off, first it's almost October. Second, do you think I can fit in a bikini without traumatizing all the fish? There will be stunned fish floating on the surface of the lake within minutes." Yeager replied.

He smiled, "You look great, as always, and we used to swim in October, as I recall." He said this softly but sincerely.

"A few weeks?" she asked.

"A few weeks," he agreed and added, "Tell Vasili and Sophia I send my best," referring to Marika's parents. "Oh, and I'll get in trouble with Jess and Tess if I don't say hi to them," he added quickly.

"You better take me to the lake! Oh, since you mentioned the ladies, I'm going to call Jess to catch up and to make sure your calendar is clear."

He rolled his eyes, bent to kiss her quickly, then left. Kostas exited security from Marika's office building, retrieved his backpack, and returned to the waiting white sedan.

"Where to, Sir?" asked the corporal.

The glow of seeing Marika quickly vanished, and his stoic demeanor returned. "The armory, corporal."

As they parked, Kostas began to exit the vehicle and said over his shoulder, "On me, corporal, bring the folder."

The young soldier quickly complied and exited the driver's seat with the folder. As they entered the armory, once again, Kostas had to clear security. As he approached the duty officer's desk, Kostas said, "Corporal Williams." Then, anticipating what Kostas was asking, the young soldier came forth and handed the folder to the duty officer marked with Top Secret in red letters.

The duty officer stood to enter a secure adjacent room where he could review the contents of the folder, then returned to where Kostas and Williams stood. "Clear all weapons currently in possession at the clearing station, then proceed."

Referring to unloading and making weapons safe. Kostas complied with the Glocks in his pack, locking the slide back after he ejected the magazine.

A few moments later, as Kostas and the Corporal proceeded down the hallway, Williams asked, "Sir?"
Kostas replied, "Yes?"

"Is this all normal in military life?" Williams asked. Undoubtedly referring to the events surrounding yesterday's attacks on the Virginia interstates.

"It depends," Kostas said.

"Sir, it depends?" asked Williams.

"If you're around me for very long," he replied.

As they continued to walk, Kostas couldn't be sure, but out of his peripheral vision, it seemed the young black soldier just turned a shade paler as they both entered the armory's storeroom.

50

Chapter 7

After obtaining NATO-compliant ammo for both his Glocks, Williams and Kostas returned to the car.

"Sir?" asked Williams.

"Yes?" replied Kostas.

"I noticed you asked for .45 full metal jacket rounds for your weapons. Is there a reason you're not using the Army's standard issue M17 pistol and 9mm ammunition?" Williams asked.

Kostas looked at him and genuinely appreciated his curiosity. He was starting to like Williams.

"Private Willaims, some of it is personal preference, some of it is technical differences between weapons. You see, the Army's M17 and M18 do have advantages for a large force like the US Army. Mainly, their interchangeable components and reliability.

However, since my first tour in Iraq, I have never been a fan of the NATO 9mm round that the Army's standard handguns are chambered in. At best, yes, it pokes holes in people, but it doesn't always put them down. Granted, the 9mm has a slightly higher kinetic energy than the .45 ACP, but the NATO-compliant round that is required by the terms of The Hague Convention of 1899, specifically, Declaration III, prohibits the use of projectiles that easily expand or flatten in the body. Hence the use of full metal jacketed ammunition.

Declaration III's requirement negates the 9mm's modern performance by requiring the full metal jacket, versus a jacketed hollow point or JHP. In a sidearm, the tried and true .45 ACP is my preferred caliber for stopping power and effective wound channels.

I only chamber my personal weapons with JHPs that will increase the size of the wound channel at impact, not just poke a hole through an intended target. It's designed to stay in the mass, not exit. After impact, the projectile creates havoc with multiple wound channels by expanding or flattening its surface area, therefore increasing mortality and the chance that the target will stay down.

I have the same opinions on the NATO .556 versus 7.62x51 or .223 and .308 in their commercial market calibers, respectively. The .556's results can be similar to the 9mm in that they both are poking holes into the targets and just poking holes through enemies that are hell bent on killing you even if that means they die also, is not effective.

Williams, two things I learned from being deployed in different sandboxes over the years are that 9mm and .556 are not as effective as .45 ACP and .762 on the battlefield.

Since I am currently performing a US Army contract, one of the requirements is that I must use NATO rounds issued in accordance with the Army's combatant engagement regulations. However, the contract mentions nothing about the make or model of the weapon that they are used in, so I pushed the caliber up since I am prohibited from using JHP and decided to use what I am comfortable with, the Glock platform.

A lesson there for you, Williams; know the exact requirements, always."

Kostas knew he had Jess to thank for that little nuance in the contract, knowing that he did not want to carry a standard-issued weapon chambered in 9mm if he could help it.

"Sir?" Williams asked again.

Kostas looked at him again, "First of all, stop calling me Sir, I am no longer in uniform. Go on." Kostas replied.

"So… you've killed someone?" Williams asked.

Kostas knew this question sat on many young soldiers, marines, and airmen's minds as they looked forward to and dreaded their first deployments. He said nothing and turned to stare through the windshield.

Chapter 8

As Williams pulled away from Dulles International Airport's departures area, Kostas walked inside to the United ticket counter. He only had his backpack and a hardshell weapons case with him. The pack contained the basic mini versions of toiletries and a change of clothes. If he needed anything else, he would buy it along the way.

After presenting his ID to the airline ticket counter, Kostas checked the locked hardshell case containing his weapons and ammunition that he obtained from the armory with the attendant. Then, he proceeded to the TSA checkpoint and the gate.

Jess had already ensured his travel arrangements to Detroit Metro Airport were secured by MGSI's travel department, including a reservation for a Hertz SUV to be ready. She did this immediately after she received the call from Kostas while he waited at the bus stop to return to the armory.

As he sat down in first class on the United Embraer 175, his mind began to wander back to Marika and all the times she wanted him to be around, but he chose differently, either because of duty or ambition.

I need to make it right with her and make some changes, he thought, as the boarding door closed, and his mind shifted back to the investigation.

How did they know? He asked himself and continued to stare out of the window at nothing in particular. Then he turned his gaze forward, closed his eyes, and began to box breathe quietly to calm his pre-takeoff nerves.

Chapter 9

Kostas Papadopoulos had no problem with engaging with an enemy in a firefight or taking risks that may result in physical harm or death, but flying was a trigger for anxiety, and he did not look forward to it.

It had become a joke of sorts over the years that big, bad Alpha from the Air Force was afraid to fly. The truth was that at one time, he had no problems flying; he went in and out of hot zones frequently while deployed over the years. Many of those flights found him sitting in nothing more than the web seating in the back of a C-130 as they performed corkscrew maneuvers to avoid enemy fire. At times, it was to avoid surface-to-air missiles, other times it was to avoid small arms fire, on occasion, both while landing in hostile or high-threat environments. Back then, he was mentally prepared for all potential scenarios going into or out of a conflict, including death.

Not long after leaving the Air Force, it only took one flight to change that forever.

It was mid-December, a windy, snowy late afternoon in Columbus, Ohio. He was booked on a flight back to Richmond after concluding a business meeting with another defense contractor a short drive north of Columbus. Kostas checked out of his room at the Renaissance Downtown and made the short trip over to the airport in the storm, anticipating delays or cancelations. He was surprised to find out the flight was on time, so he settled into the small terminal bar and ordered a Guinness.

When the boarding call came, he finished his draft and scanned his boarding pass. After settling into his seat, the captain informed the passengers that they would have to de-ice before takeoff, so there would be a slight delay in departure, but he felt confident they would make up the time in flight. Kostas peered out the windows at the equipment de-icing the plane on both sides and flipped through the Delta Sky magazine for no particular reason other than it was there.

They taxied away from the deicing station and waited a few more minutes before turning to the runway. Apparently waiting for clearance to take off, he started to doze off.

As the plane turned, and he felt the engines surge, he woke up as the aircraft gained weight off the wheels, the feeling of the plane just leaving just leaving contact with the ground. They must have only been a few feet separated from the landing gear and the concrete when he felt the entire plane jerk violently to the left, then straighten, then again. From experience in his Air Force career, he was well aware of what was happening.

The two-engine aircraft's number one engine produced several compressor stalls just feet from the ground at almost 160 miles an hour. The craft had passed the V1 speed, or the decision speed, the critical point of no return, where the takeoff cannot be aborted. Either you get airborne, or you crash.

Kostas was intimately familiar with the airport's surrounding community, which consisted of a mix of hotels, restaurants, and office buildings, some ironically belonging to the Department of Defense. He knew the direction they were taking off from would result in him being violently checked in against his will in the airport's Best Western with his current oversized luggage of a Delta commuter jet and all the souls on board if the pilot didn't get this right.

Kostas glanced to his right, a glow of an orange light behind him, and the smell of burning jet fuel mixed with other distinct odors that came from an engine on fire.

As the flight attendants were running around saying Hail-Marys and Our Fathers, the captain seemingly mistook the PA System that broadcasts to the passengers in the cabin for the plane's interphone used to communicate between the pilots and flight attendants. Next, the passengers heard the pilot's voice asking, "Is the fire inside or outside?" over the plane's PA system.

Nothing will instill panic in a human being like being asked that question while a handful of feet off the ground at over 140 knots and hotels quickly approaching in a snowstorm. The pilot evidently remembered his emergency procedures then, chopping the fuel on the engine that was ablaze and allowing the rush of air and lack of jet fuel to extinguish the fire as he took the number two throttle to the wall. The plane began to rise as Kostas viewed the last light of the runway that he could swear was only a few yards from the aircraft.

As the craft continued to gain altitude, the captain returned to the PA system, this time intentionally: "Folks, we are okay."

Comforting, Kostas thought, but not believing it.

The captain continued, "The plane has two engines for safety reasons; it is designed to fly with one."

Kostas had a brand-new admiration for F-16 pilots, who only had a single engine.

"ATC," or air traffic control, "has cleared the airspace for us. It will take approximately twelve minutes to get back on the ground, " the captain added.

Those seemed the longest twelve minutes of Kostas's life. Should he violate all FAA regulations and text Marika, or call her from his cellphone? A thousand things went through his mind in an instant. Kostas had never been religious, despite being born and baptized into the Greek-Orthodox Church. He subscribed to taking the agnostic approach as his grandfather did, be moral, have an ethos. Don't rely on knowing who God is or isn't, nor believing in the dogmas of mankind's organized religion. Since he took a more pragmatic view of God, praying was out of the question, and Marika is all he thought of.

After what seemed more like twelve hours, not twelve minutes, the plane touched down on the runway. Kostas watched the oddly appropriate dance of red strobe lights from the emergency chase vehicles bouncing off the snow-covered airfield; it was Christmas after all.

As the plane slowed, there was silence in the cabin; the only sound was the noise of the single working engine. No passenger or crew member said a word. Kostas looked around, and in military-style gallows humor, projected his voice. He broke the silence, "Well, I don't know about any of you, but I'm a Michigan Wolverine and have never been so happy to be on the ground in Columbus, Ohio!" Some people burst out laughing, others cried, and some a mixture of both.

As with many traumatic events, the effects are not immediate; you return to normal, even overcompensate, until the gravity of the situation hits and the adrenaline is gone. After that comes the emotional crash and the aftermath that can stick with a person for years.

The next morning, he woke up in the same room he had checked out of the day before, showered, then took an Uber to the airport. Kostas made his way through security, and then it hit him like a kick to the chest. The smell of something burning, his hands started to sweat, his heart started beating so fast he thought he was in cardiac arrest. He felt weak and collapsed to one knee on the terminal's tile floor, then sat against a wall. In the terminal's only restaurant that was open for breakfast, a cook had evidently burned a customer's morning toast, and that's all it took, the smell.

There it was… his first acknowledged panic attack due to a traumatic event. Thanks to training in SERE and High-Risk Capture, he was mentally prepared for every worst-case scenario that could happen while on a mission when he was still in uniform. That one fateful night in Columbus, no longer in uniform, he was not mentally prepared. Now, his mental world had a small fissure in it that would allow the rest of the trauma he witnessed during his life to seep into his consciousness.

At the time of his transition out of uniform, the military and the VA did little to encourage personnel or veterans to get mental health help. It was all tag lines and posters hung up in hallways. Few veterans were willing to risk involuntary separation due to mental health issues or a security clearance being revoked. Even after separation from the military, there was a serious risk of not keeping security clearances if you were diagnosed with PTSD by the VA, and few were willing to throw away lucrative job opportunities with defense contractors or even Government Agencies to seek treatment.

Like most veterans, Kostas pushed everything down and moved on, systematically completing each mission or task at hand. Emotions were not an issued piece of authorized equipment; they didn't have a national stock number like almost everything else in the military.

Kostas continued his ritual of preflight Box Breathing during takeoff from Dulles. In his mind, he paraphrased a line from Marcus Aurelius's Meditations ... "Remove emotion from the mind, not the heart." He repeated it three more times, then placed his Bose noise-canceling headphones on his head and pressed play on his audiobook app. He then continued where he left off in the latest David Baldacci novel featuring the character Will Robie.

Chapter 10

Once back on the ground at Detroit Metro Airport, Kostas deplaned and made his way to the McNamara Terminal, walking into the main terminal on his right. The large bank of panels on which the airport streamed live television was tuned to CNN, showing a presidential candidate during a campaign rally. As Kostas walked by, he heard "there will be a bloodbath if I'm not elected…"

Kostas continued walking and wondered why he even tried anymore after hearing a potential leader of the nation spout rhetoric like that.

He made a right at the Arrival and Departure screens and stopped at the Brooks Brothers, located in the terminal before the baggage claim area. There, he picked out an off-the-rack dark charcoal gray sport coat that was one size too large for him.

An attractive college-age sales attendant approached him with a smile and asked if he would like to be measured and maybe have the coat tailored and shipped. He replied, "No."

Understanding that the young saleswoman was likely looking for an opportunity to upsell pants, shirts, and ties, and any other accessory she could convince him of.

"I'll take this," he said.

Surprised by the sudden and short reply, she said, "I can show you some matching slacks."

"No, thank you. I'll wear it, no need to bag it."

"Here you go miss." He said, handing her his American Express Card.

Her expression changed, visibly showing that she was disappointed with the missed opportunity for an upsell and a larger commission, she took the card without a word. She returned shortly after with his receipt and his card.

"Thank you," he said, folding the coat over his arm. He then made his way out of the store and to baggage claim, where he retrieved the locked hardshell case. After inspecting the case for damage or compromise, he went to the men's room.

Once inside, he entered an unoccupied stall, hung his backpack on one hook and his new sports coat on another. He placed the case on the commode, then swapped his black company-logoed shirt for an identical shirt without any logo.

Once he returned the previous shirt to the pack, he donned the black shoulder rig holster and one of the two Glocks that were contained in the black hardshell case. He then placed two magazines into the right side magazine holders and secured them with the straps and snaps. He would later rack a round into the chamber once he was safe from anyone hearing it, creating unnecessary panic in the terminal.

Then he removed the other already holstered Glock, the smaller of the two models, from the case and placed the holster in the small of his back, clipping it to his belt. Kostas then slipped on the new sports coat, concealing his arsenal, and thought the jacket wasn't old man Franco's, but it would *do*. Slinging the backpack over one shoulder and grabbing the case, he exited the stall and walked directly to the shuttle for the Hertz lot.

Walking in a stride of purpose, Kostas exited the shuttle as soon as it came to a stop, then walked directly to the blue SUV that Jess had arranged for him. He placed his pack in the passenger seat next to him. He performed a habitual safety check, not for damage that may be present on the vehicle before rental, but for any devices that may cause him harm or track his movements. Once back in the SUV, he removed each pistol one at a time, racking a round into each chamber, then ejecting each magazine from the weapons. He reached into the pack and took out a box of ammunition, removed two .45 caliber rounds, and returned the box to the pack. Kostas replaced the missing rounds from each magazine that were now housed in each gun's chamber, then returned the weapons to their respective holsters.

He punched in the address for Rizzarreo's wife's last known address into his navigation app and placed his phone in the cup holder, then exited the airport on I-94 East for the roughly hour-long drive to a small Michigan town, specifically the surrounding area known as Muttonville.

With a population of just under six thousand residents, located in the eastern part of the state, just north of Lake St. Clair, he knew from the research Jess provided him that it was another economically depressed part of the state with primarily white residents. Historically, an area that was once known for its slaughterhouses that served the area's sheep farmers.

Chapter 11

Kostas turned off Interstate 94 and onto Country Line Rd. After a few more turns on several gravel roads, he arrived at a dilapidated old two-story white farmhouse surrounded by overgrown vegetation with a singlewide out back that was barely visible from the road. The mailbox was removed, only a post at the gravel driveway, but the GPS said it was the place. He drove the SUV two-thirds of the way up the long gravel drive, then parked and waited to see any signs of occupants. While waiting, he did note what looked to be a basic pistol and rifle range situated from the back of the singlewide and off into a fallow field. The shooter placements were constructed of 2x4s, and the wooden target posts showed wear and extensive use.

The door on the singlewide trailer slowly opened, and a small child, maybe the age of seven or eight, made her way down the crudely constructed steps of cinderblocks. The girl wearing dirty jeans and a ripped Kenny Chesney concert T-shirt that looked to be two sizes too large for her walked into what could only be generously called a yard, then stopped. Kostas checked all the rearview mirrors in the SUV to clear his six o'clock position before pocketing the keys and exiting the vehicle. As Kostas walked closer to the girl who seemed to be stuck at an invisible line in the weeds, he noticed one of the windows of the trailer open partially next to the door, and a thin, almost transparent curtain fabric was slightly waving in the breeze.

"Hi," he said. The little girl did not respond. "Is your mother home?" he added. The little girl shook her head no. "Do you know when she will be home?" he asked. Again, a headshake no. Kostas noticed a new shadow behind the window's curtain. "Okay," he said while still walking toward the little girl. "Could you give her a message?" he said with a smile, still approaching the girl. Another head shake, no. "If I wrote it down?" he added. He was now within five yards of the girl.

"STOP! If you make one move or step any closer to the girl, you will have a new hole where you don't want one," a gruff woman's voice said from the window.

Kostas slowly placed his hands in the air and simultaneously lowered to one knee, appearing as if he would lie down on his belly. Instead, he stopped with his right knee on the ground and his left still up, placing him in an easy position to draw his Glock from the shoulder rig.

"I'm with the Department of the Army, I can pull my ID out if you will agree not to shoot me while doing it, it's in my right coat pocket," he said. A long silence fell. he added, "It's about your husband..."

"You FEDs killed him," came the reply. There were now tears running down the little girl's face.

"I'm not a FED, I'm Army," he lied.

"What's the Army got to do with all this?" came the response from the Texas accent in the window.

Kostas had to use a variant of good cop, bad cop. "Thankfully, the Army got the lead on this and not those guys down in Quantico that are up the FBI's ass." he retorted. Silence again. "I just want to talk, I was active duty at one time also, I want to understand what happened to Gerraldo." he knew what happened, he pulled the trigger that caused him to take his own life. "And not let the FEDs twist what happened to a fellow veteran in their own interest," he added.

"They lied! The FBI and the news said he killed himself! He wouldn't do that! Not to us! They killed him!" again, from the thick Texas accent.

"I understand, that's why I'm here to find out the truth, can I pull out my credentials?" Kostas asked.

"Beth-Ann, get in here now! " The woman yelled. Let's see it! Throw it to Beth-Ann!" He did. The little girl picked it up from the weeds and dirt and ran into the house.

"How do you say your name?" the window asked.

"Kostas, Kostas Papadopoulos," he responded.

"Whatever, and you are a Vet? With a name like that?" The window asked a bit incredulously.

"Yes, ma'am, born and raised here in Michigan. Dearborn, to be exact, went to Edsel Ford High School before I joined the military, my father was Greek."

"Greektown? I like going to them casinos," the window replied.

This recurring misconception plagued all Greeks living in the Detroit metropolitan area of Michigan. Once a non-Greek found out you were from lower Michigan, they automatically associated you with Greektown, known for the historic district located in the heart of Detroit and its rich cultural heritage. Due to the restaurants, entertainment, and the Greektown Casino-Hotel, it is one of the city's most popular attractions for both locals and visitors.

"Close to there, yes," he allowed. Can you throw me back my ID?" Kostas asked. She did, and it landed a few feet from the window. He used this opportunity to get closer. As he picked up the ID pack, he started, "ma'am, I am trying to make sure the FBI doesn't misrepresent the facts here."

"That's all they do, lie, lie, lie! Gerry was a good man, God fearing patriot, and was willing to fight for his country, and still was. Them liars are ruining this country and now they killed Gerry! First the border, then cheat'n at elections! Lawrence and Red have the right of it! The whole country has gone to shit and now Gerry is gone!" she sobbed. Kostas made a mental note of the references to Lawrence and Red.

Do you know why Gerry was there in the Capital region? He asked.

"Sum'tin to do with a campaign rally, support'n the right of it." She said.

"The right of it?" Kostas asked.

"That's right, Mr. Whittaker's campaign, ya know I saw him once here in Michigan, we drove three hours, Gerry and I, to support him at a rally years ago. Got right up front, and Mr. Whittiker smiled right at me and gave me a thumbs up. I just about fell over, I was so excited. Mr. Whittaker will put it right, you'll see. Rob him of an election, it ain't right! Them FEDs that killed Gerry, they will get theirs, I promise you!" and then she started sobbing again.

"I'm sorry, ma'am. I want to help. Could you tell me if he was going to meet anyone there? Did he go there with someone, maybe a group?" Kostas asked.

"You asking for the FBI?" the window sniffed.

"No, ma'am. The Department of Defense, the same one that Gerry served honorably in." Another *lie*, he thought to himself, "no matter what the FEDs say. I just want to help." Kostas replied.

"He was supposed to meet Andy at the Cabela's down on US23. They were going to drive together. Ya know Andy is a vet too, he got screwed just like Gerry, they took his promotion away from him for no reason, no reason at all. He's a colonel, would have been a General if them liberal sons of a bitches weren't allowed to run around the country like they do, homosexuals and child molesters for gods sakes! Mr. Whittaker will take care of 'em, he promised!" she proclaimed.

"'eh, yes ma'am. Do you know where I can find Andy?" he asked. A long silence and the window closed, and he could hear more sobbing.

Chapter 12

Kostas headed west on I-94 back to the airport, it was 5:55 p.m. He used the speakerphone on his cell to call Wade, avoiding the paired link between his phone and the rental car.

"You're early for once," came Wade's voice.

"I figured I would update you before the flight back to Dulles, " he replied. Kostas filled Wade in on the details of the conversation with McMoore, noting both the names Lawrence and Red and the context in which she spoke about them.

"Anything else?" Wade asked.

"Yeah, a former colonel who separated due to a red line on his promotion, the only name I have is Andy. Supposably Rizzarreo and Andy were to meet at the Cabela's off US23 and drive together to a campaign rally somewhere in Virginia."

Kostas added, "I would ask the State Police to sit on McMoore for a few days and maybe let Hogan know. I got the impression it's a small town, and the locals may or may not cooperate fully."

"I'll call Hogan and have the analyst team comb through DEERS and MPRS for any redlined promotions in the last ten years at O6 to start," replied Wade, referring to the Department of Defense's systems of record for military personnel and benefit records.

"Exactly what I was thinking," said Kostas. "Also, something else came up, Whittaker," he added.

"Shit" came back the reply.

"Yep"

"Once you get back to Virginia, let's talk about that in a more comfortable environment," Wade said.

"Copy" was his only response. For the remainder of the drive to DTW, Kostas thought in silence with nothing more than the sound of the interstate.

Kostas returned the rental to Hertz and made his way to the shuttle to the terminal. Once seated, he called Jess. "Any updates? he asked.

"Some, there have been some information requests on you and MGSI."

"From who?" Kostas asked, alarmed.

"I'm not completely certain, but it seems like rookie investigators for the FBI or law enforcement," Jess replied.

"See if you can ask JP for a favor and see what he can come up with on those inquires." Kostas instructed.

Referring to James Pope, a long time close friend who served with Kostas in the Air Force until he lost his left eye in the line of duty shortly after 911, now he was an analyst at the Defense Intelligence Agency.

Jess asked, "Isn't the DIA already involved with the investigation?"

"Yes, but something is telling me not to go through official channels on this request. Call his home line to see if he wants to meet for coffee off the books."

Let's sync back up when I get back to Richmond," he replied.

Not wanting him to hang up, she quickly broke in, "There is one more thing. I am sorry..." As another call was dialing in, he looked at the screen; it was Marika.

"Jess, is there something I should know?" Kostas asked Jess after looking at the caller ID on the screen.

She replied, "Call me back when you're off that call coming in, and again, sorry." She then hung up.

With more than a little foreboding feeling creeping from his stomach to his head, he clicked over to the incoming call, "Hello?"

It was Marika's voice; her not happy with him voice, "WHAT THE HELL KOSTAS?" she continued without skipping a breath, "Jess told me you were on I-95, what the hell?"

Kostas thought to himself, *"So much for the intel officer in Jess; the West End and kids' soccer have made her soft."*

She continued, "And don't you dare come down on Jess for this! I called to make sure your calendar was clear for the lake trip you promised me!" she continued, "WHAT THE HELL, KOSTAS?"

The next words were a mix of illegible Greek and English curses with an extra portion of insults, but he did catch a brief bit in Greek: "I'll make you eat wood." Referring to a poor direct translation of a threat to a child in trouble from a parent.

"I didn't want to ruin the mood in your office?" he said in a sort of a plea for leniency.

"Damn you! You could have been killed!" she said, giving him no quarter.

"I wasn't," he said simply but reassuringly.

"But..." she started; Kostas cut her off.

"I'm okay," he paused. *I was in the wrong place at the wrong time, nothing more. It is over, and the only casualty to me personally was the Explorer. I'm okay, Marika."* He paused again. "I miss you," he finished.

He then heard a slight sniffle over the line. "Hey, I'm getting ready to fly back to Virginia, can we talk later?" he said softly to break up the silence and sniffles.

"Dulles?" she asked.

"Dulles," he answered. "Out of Detroit," he added.

"Really? Is it family?" she asked now, unconcerned with the I-95 situation.

"No, you know better than that," he replied softly.

"I'm leaving Belvoir as soon as I get off the phone with you. See you in arrivals." Then she was gone.

He dialed Jess back, and before she could say hello, he said, "You're getting soft, Jess," as he sat down on the plane.

"I know, I know, I'm sorry but you two are so good together, and besides, I thought she knew that you were on I-95 during the attack," she replied sheepishly; now it was Jess's turn to beg for quarter.

"They're closing the boarding door. Get our analysts on the leads for Andy, Lawrence, and Red. Wade's office will have additional information. I'll see you tomorrow." With that, he ended the call.

Chapter 13

Kostas exited the automatic doors from the arrivals area and walked to the curb. A few moments later, a red Subaru Solterra pulled near and beeped its horn. He tossed his backpack and case into the rear seat and entered the passenger side.

Kostas said to the driver, "With all that money you make on your line of yoga clothes, I thought you could at least own a Ford," digging into his repertoire of frequent teases about Marika's first name. This particular one targeted at the coincidence of a clothes designer for high-end yoga outfits that shares the same name.

Marika quipped, "Funny, if I were that Marika, do you think I would still be putting time into getting my retirement from the Air Force? Now get in the car, Mr. Funny boy, and you're still in trouble." She pulled away from the curb and into traffic.

"Should I expect a punishment?" he asked with a hopeful tone.

"No! I know you'll like it too much," she quipped back. "You're stuck with dinner and a long ride to Richmond from me," she added.

"I appreciate it, but I have to get in to see Wade," he replied.

"You're in luck. I'm taking you to Belvoir now, and tomorrow morning, we are going to Richmond together. Wade is waiting for you at his office; dinner will be later tonight," she said in a tone that told him the rest was not up for negotiation.

Kostas sat and wondered, did everyone exclude him from details in his personal life at this point? Jess, Marika, Wade?

He had fully expected Corporal Williams to pick him up at Dulles and take him back to Belvoir to talk with Wade and return him to Richmond later that night. Seems the three closest people in his life took matters into their own hands at this point.

Is the universe trying to tell my old ass something? He pondered mentally as they drove down the Dulles Access Road.

Marika broke the silence, "No time to see her?"

"Who?" Kostas asked. He knew where this was going and didn't care for it.

"Stop it, your mother," she said in a disapproving tone.

"No," was his only reply. Then he took out his phone to text Wade's number, saying, "I'm likely forty minutes out," and hit send.

Kostas's parents split up after almost twenty years of marriage when he and his younger brother Dimitri were still in school. At the time, Kostas was a senior in high school, and Dimetri was in junior high. It was no surprise; his parents fought all the time, for as long as Kostas could remember. His mother was physically violent to both Kostas and his father. Once Loretta took a hot metal spatula that she had been cooking with and hit his father on the upper arm. The resulting burn mark looked to resemble an "L" due to the angle she had struck him at. Later, she bragged that she branded him with the "L" for Loretta.

His father wasn't an example of the most upstanding human being either. An egomaniac who thrived on attention from younger women and was always trying to get over on someone, be it a business partner or the government, he was always looking for an angle to his benefit with little regard for others. Kostas and Demitri would joke about the fact that they had two great examples of what not to become in life. Both brothers became successful in their respective careers and their lives.

The memory burned into both Kostas's and Dimetri's minds of their mother Loretta stabbing Kostas in his left arm with a screwdriver when the two argued. Kostas was seventeen. The physical abuse wasn't as bad as the mental aftermath.

Loretta had circled the wagons around protecting her nursing license, and her only comment to Kostas was, "I could have lost my license if I wasn't lucky enough to have the social workers see it from my point of view."

With no hint of regret or apology in her voice or demeanor, Kostas left right then and rented rooms from friends until he was out of high school and joined the Air Force at age eighteen, never looking back.

Marika's SUV entered Fort Belvoir through the John J. Kingman gate and drove a short distance to the building where Wade's office was located. She dropped off Kostas at the front door. "Text me when you're ready. I'm going over to the Class Six," she said, referring to the on-post liquor store and the Commissary. Do you need anything?"

"Not that I can think of, thanks. I shouldn't be long." Kostas replied.

He entered Wade's office, and Corporal Williams sat in the reception area near the aide's desk. Kostas greeted him, "Williams," with a head nod.

"Sir... eh..." Williams began.

"Call me Kostas or Alpha, either is fine. I am no longer in uniform. Also, I won't need transportation tonight, go home and get a good night's sleep." Kostas said in a level but slightly warm tone.

"Yes, Sir... ah... Kostas." The young corporal finally came up with.

Wade's aide showed him into the General's office and asked if he needed anything.

"Water, please," Kostas replied. The aide ran after a bottle of water and returned with it for Kostas.

Looking up from his computer and standing to shake Kostas's hand, Wade said to the aide, "That will be all." The aide closed the door as he left the room.

After returning to his desk, Wade asked, "Whittaker?" Kostas nodded. "Are you sure?"

"One hundred percent," Kostas replied.

"Shit" Wade let out slowly. "Do you think he's involved directly?" he added.

Kostas replied, "It's Hard to say at this point; I'm leaving all options on the table."

Wade slowly nodded. "I read the rest of your notes from the widow. Do you think she knows anything else?"

"Not likely, she is just an unfortunate soul who's too simple to understand the world around her—getting her news from social media sites and foreign-designed bots that know her profile and past clicks. Those sites continuously feed her and others around the country articles with the red meat of the domestic extremists and disinformation from Russia, China, and North Korea. She's a sad soul in a sad world of her own with no escape."

He paused, "Have the state cops gotten any leads from the surveillance?" Kostas asked.

"A few texts, mostly condolences on her loss. No calls, just more garbage on social media, but the FBI is tracking that, she hasn't left the trailer."

Wade turned back to his emails on the computer and said, "Nobody in, nobody out, nothing to note. They are still watching her movements and comms."

"You may want to contact the local law enforcement to get someone to do a wellness check on the kid. Make sure she's at least at school." Kostas added.

"Like I said, no one in or out since you left. I'll make a call for the check." Wade said.

"How is the joint task force going? Everyone playing nice in the sandbox?" Kostas asked.

"In short, no. Homeland Security and the FBI are still pissed at the highest levels and still want to lead the investigation themselves. NSA and DIA are scared to reveal too much intelligence. Therefore, they are not helpful at all. It's still a shit show in the Capital. Without our involvement in Project Paratiro, the SecDef and the rest of the DoD would have been happy to flick this booger on someone else's windshield and let them manage it. As a matter of fact, the FBI should be in the conference room soon. I'll see you in there. Give me a few minutes to answer these emails." Wade replied, then yelled for his aide.

As Kostas stood from the chair, he asked, "How much of Muttonville are you keeping out of circulation?"

"Almost all of it concerning W," Wade replied, referring to Whittaker.

"But I won't be able to keep a lid on that long. I just let the 'needs-to-knows' in on what you observed with the rifle range and the widow's responses about her husband and "Andy." I excluded all W references. What's your next move?" he added.

"Dinner, Richmond, then some research on Andy, Lawrence, and Red."

"Dinner with Marika?" Wade asked.

Kostas nodded.

"Good, glad to see it."

"Hey, Wade, it would be helpful if DHS and the FBI would send MGSI their files on each of them. They must be known to someone. After that, who knows, maybe a good old-fashioned raid to send a message and shake a few trees to see what comes loose. Do I have resources from you?"

"Yes, but you can't lead any raids as a defense contractor; Hogan will have to take the lead on that. You know, it would be much easier if you were still in uniform." Wade replied.

"Well, I have work to do." Kostas trailed off, ending the conversation as he grabbed his bottle of water and exited to the hallway.

Chapter 14

Kostas exited Wade's office reception area and went to the small conference room across the hallway. Agent Hogan was waiting, seated at the conference table with a large file in front of her.

He sat opposite her, then greeted her, "Agent Hogan." She smiled and opened the folder in front of her.

Hogan smiled thinly and cleared her throat, "Konstantinos, also known as Kostas, Papadopoulos. Age fifty-one. Born in Dearborn Michigan to a Loretta and Nickolas Papadopoulos, the latter deceased. One sibling, a Dimitri Papadopoulos, age forty-eight, a Boeing Executive, married with two children.

In high school, you were an average student, then an above-average athlete in football and wrestling."

She paused to turn a page, "Entered into the delayed enlistment program at the age of seventeen during the early days of Desert Shield. At age eighteen entered into active military service with the United States Air Force in the Bioenvironmental Engineering career field, where you graduated at the top of your class. First duty station McDill AFB. Shortly thereafter applied for the Air Force's bootstrap program to move from enlisted to the officer ranks. Top scores in the Air Force Officer Qualification Test."

She looked up at him with a thin smile, then continued, "Big move for a blue-collar kid like you. You then attended the University of Michigan to complete a degree in Chemical Engineering with a minor in Public Policy; in under three years, impressive." She smirked with an approving nod of her head, then continued, "Commissioned as a second lieutenant after completing Officer Training School, head of graduating class, and served two years as OIC at Shaw AFB's Chem-Bio Office."

Faking surprise, she continued, "My-my, while in the Air Force, three deployments into Kuwait. Volunteered for the 609th Air Operations Group, four more deployments between Iraq and Afghanistan, totaling twenty-eight months. Not home much, are you?"

She turned another page, "Detailed to DTRA from the 609th for a DoD-funded joint-purple team program known as Program Paratiro. Two more deployments to Afghanistan. Combat decorated, two Purple Hearts, two Bronze Stars with V devices, then a Navy Cross."

She paused and looked up at him, then said, "For a fly boy like you, you must have done something really special for the Navy to take notice of you, not being a Special Forces Operator as you claim."

"As I told you, I'm more of an analyst."

"More like a mercenary, as I told you." She corrected with a scoff, then continued, "Odd though, with all those accolades, you only obtained the rank of Major. Why is that?"

"Personality conflicts."

Laughing sarcastically, she said, "I bet!" Then she continued, "It was more like a disciplinary action, an Article 15, non-judicial punishment that I found in the record. It was redacted from the official file after someone noticed some, let's call them irregularities in the prosecution's case, but you know how it is: Nothing can ever be truly removed forever from a US Government file.

Moving on. Like most of your deployments and metals, the narratives are heavily redacted. However, I did find a beryllium exposure report that resulted in the lymph nodes of your chest area being surrounded by an abnormal amount of scar tissue. Doctors initially thought you may have had leukemia in your mid-thirties." She paused and looked up at him. "Ok… one, that's scary as hell. Two, how did you get exposed to beryllium? "

"It's sometimes called Manhattan Project Syndrome."

"That doesn't answer the question."

Locking eyes with her and with a stone-faced expression, he said, "Beryllium, or atomic number four on the periodic table, is a key component in the manufacturing of nuclear weapons, among other things. During the Manhattan Project, the dangers of beryllium dust were not well known, and workers were obviously in a rush to develop the weapon. So, for the most part, they were not adequately protected. My symptoms are emblematic of those on the Manhattan Project."

"Still doesn't answer the question."

"Agent Hogan, you know my background obviously, so I am sure you can infer where and how I was exposed."

She looked back down at the file, coughed, then continued, "You have shrapnel in your mid-right abdomen from an AK-47 round that exploded when the weapon went out of battery. The surgeon decided not to remove it. The procedure would likely cause more damage than leaving it." Again, a pause and a quizzical look from her, "And why were you firing an AK-47?" she asked.

"Seemed like the right thing to do at the time," is all he said.

She made a small laugh while shaking her head and resumed, "Fusion of C4, C5, and C6 vertebrae with a titanium cage around the neck. Total reconstructive surgery of the right shoulder, a SLAP procedure… whatever that means. The surgery included reattaching one head of the bicep to the shoulder. Seems this was all due to a single event, an IED explosion that resulted in you being thrown against a concrete wall."

"Superior Labrum from Anterior to Posterior." He interrupted.

"What?" Hogan asked.

"SLAP, a Superior Labrum from Anterior to Posterior repair of the shoulder to reattach a torn labrum back to the socket of the shoulder joint," Kostas replied.

"Sounds painful."

"Not really. And it was a concrete pillar, not a wall." He responded with no emotion in his voice or on his face.

She coughed uncomfortably and started again: " You voluntarily left your commission to separate from the Air Force. The first letter of resignation of your commission was officially declined, with no explanation. After resubmission, it was approved by the same Brigadier General that declined it... odd." Again, she looked at him quizzically.

"Change of heart," Kostas replied before she could ask.

Hogan then added, "Why all of a sudden and so quickly?"

"You would have to ask him,"

With another tilt of her head, that she evidently thought at this point was endearing or disarming, she continued, "Started Meraki Government Solutions Incorporated or MGSI, in Richmond, Virginia."

Again, she paused, locked eyes with him, and added, "You have done well for yourself for a so-called analyst." With a smug tone that was a little accusatory.

"A downtown office overlooking the James River and Brown's Island. A nice house on the prestigious Monument Avenue. Too bad they tore down the monuments, I heard the real estate value really took a hit."

"You mean the row of second place trophies?" Kostas asked.

"What?" Hogan asked, perplexed.

"Second place trophies, the Confederacy lost the war. In my estimation, the value of the area went up considerably after their removal." He quipped back at her.

She took a moment to think carefully about her next words then continued after looking down at the file, "Two ex-wife's, first the typical "military starter marriage" with a local woman looking to better her options in life. No different from 90 percent of young military enlistees' marriages," she shrugged, "crash and burn nothing new there. Second marriage, married military-to-military, again crash and burn." she looked up at Kostas, "Trying to fix your childhood with your own marriages Alpha? Fix what your parents failed at?"

He said nothing.

She looked back at the file again, regained the small smile on her face, and said, "It looks like you have wife number three in your sights."

"If that's an offer, no thanks," he replied deadpan.

She answered with a matching mocking tone and a seductive grin, "Why haven't you even bought me dinner yet, Kostas?" Then, she fluttered her eyes in an equally mocking gesture.

She continued, "I'm referring to an on-again, off-again long relationship with a Lieutenant Colonel Marika Yeager. Coincidentally, here on Belvoir, it looks like she requested a change of assignment for her last duty station before retirement. Odd… she recently received a line number for a promotion to full bird colonel."

Again, the tilt of the head, "Did you know that?" Not waiting for an answer she wasn't going to get, she continued, "Looks like she might have wanted to get closer to you, at least geographically speaking, or maybe not just geographically speaking. "She mocked with a teasing tone.

"You would have to ask her," he replied.

"I don't think that will be necessary; I know women, Kostas, and I know how women think. In addition to being one, just in case you didn't notice, I'm also a trained investigator, remember? That's what the FBI pays me for, putting clues together. I'm confident that she's not here in Virginia for the golf courses at Belvoir; she doesn't golf." She laughed in a superior and an I know everything tone.

"And you know that how?" Kostas interjected.

"What, that she doesn't golf?" Hogan asked.

"Yes, you checked her out?"

Hogan shrugged with an impish grin and replied, "Seemed relevant to your file."

"What does my file and all of this have to do with investigating a domestic terrorist attack on American soil?" Kostas asked.

"That's what I am trying to find out," she replied, her eyes narrowing in on him. Then, after a long pause added, "Here you are in General Wade Morris's office; redacted witness N224. Why?"

"Ask General Morris, he's in charge," he replied, again in a deadpan tone.

As that last statement hung in the resulting silence, they stared coldly at each other. Wade entered the room, and both Kostas and Hogan stood at attention. Kostas used this opportunity to leave the room, telling Wade on the way out, "I'll report in tomorrow morning, General. I believe Agent Hogan has a question for you." Then he exited the room into the hallway.

Chapter 15

Kostas climbed into Marika's car, which was waiting outside the four-story office complex, which was an addition to a larger existing building originally constructed for a Defense Agency headquarters on Belvoir.

He lapsed into silence as he thought about the encounter with Hogan. *Why was Hogan trying to get under his skin? Why mess with me? Any problem with Wade's office leading the investigation should be left at Wade's feet, not his.*

"Everything go all right?" asked Marika, bringing Kostas back from his thoughts.

"Yeah, yeah, Wade says hi." He recovered with.

As they drove to Marika's townhouse, Kostas returned to his thoughts: *What is Hogan's game here? Her motivation? It can't be just a turf war with the DoD since they are leading the investigation and not the FBI, can it?*

As he pondered the problem rolling around in his mind, a moment of clarity struck him. There were two more possibilities. But which one was the right answer?

It was a short trip to the townhouse at that time of night. Marika pulled into the narrow two-car garage on the ground floor of the townhome, then exited her car and popped the hatch for the back. Kostas grabbed his backpack and two reusable cloth bags full of items, one of which was a wine carrier.

"What's for dinner?" he asked.

"You're in luck!" she replied with a grin. "Trader Joe's frozen mushroom flatbreads from my freezer,"

"Then what's with all of this?" presenting the two bags with outstretched arms.

"For Jess and Tess. Jess asked me to bring down some of her PX favorites since she can't get them in Richmond." Referring to the Post Exchange.

"Two of those bottles of wine are for us."

"Well, at least there is a silver lining to me being the pack mule... wine." He said with a grin that matched hers.

Kostas opened a bottle of wine, grabbed the two pizzas from the freezer, and turned the oven on to preheat.

"Wow no screw top." He exclaimed.

"Nothing but the best corked eleven-dollar bottle of wine for you, we are not exactly at your place with a stocked cellar." She said with a wink.

Continuing, "Remember, I'm still on Uncle Sam's payroll, not a big-shot government contractor." She replied with another wink to the grin she already had.

They caught up on lost time as they shared the wine and ate the two pizzas that were quartered into slices. Kostas asked about Marika's parents and her brother. She asked about Dimetri, Kostas' brother, his wife, and kids.

"Isabella is the doting mother as always, Daniela is a star swimmer for her age group, and John is a chip off Dimetri's block, a great hockey player. Dimetri is doing well." Kostas reported, then he picked up the wine bottle and shook it, showing it was empty.

"Another?" He asked.

"Hell no!" Marika replied, looking at him like he had lost his mind. "It's late, and tomorrow will come early, and besides…" She paused as she stood up from the couch to take the plates to the kitchen.

"Besides what?" Kostas asked.

She smiled and winked, "You have work to do."

Kostas grabbed the empty bottle of wine, placed it in the kitchen recycling bin, and saluted her in a playful show of 'as-you-wish.' Then followed her to the bedroom.

Chapter 16

The next morning, as the slivers of sunlight had just started peeking through the window blinds, they both lay there, Marika's head on his chest and his arm around her. "I miss you." She whispered.

"I miss you too," Kostas replied.

As they had done so many mornings in the past, without a word being said, he rolled over to his side, and she began to scratch his back lightly, which she knew he loved. After a few light scratches, she used her index finger to outline the two tattoos that Kostas got back in his early twenties, first on his right shoulder blade. It depicted a black Maltese cross with an inscription in Greek: 'THE COURAGE TO ACT, THE ABILITY TO RESPOND, AND THE DESIRE TO SERVE.'

Then she outlined the one on the left shoulder blade, a black diamond shape with a cross extending from the bottom point of the diamond. The symbol represented Athena, the Greek goddess of wisdom, knowledge, and war. Inscribed around it, 'I SEARCH THE TRUTH; I FIND THE TRUTH.'

Kostas broke the silence, "Oh, by the way, congratulations." She stopped tracing the outlines on his back.

"That's a big accomplishment, O-6. I am sure your parents are enormously proud. I'm proud of you being promoted." He finished.

"Who told you?" she asked.

"Word gets around fast. You must be excited." He dodged the source of the information.

"It's getting late, traffic is going to be horrible." She said, quickly changing the subject, then got up out of the bed and walked over to the en suite bathroom. He was used to her abruptly changing the subject in a conversation when it was something she did not want to talk about. He heard the shower start. Kostas rolled out of bed, dressed, and went to the kitchen. Once the coffee was ready in the French press, he poured the steaming liquid into two travel mugs he found in a corner cabinet.

"No shower?" Marika asked.

"I used your kitchen sink, " he teased, and she smiled. "Like you said, it's getting late. I'll shower at the office once I get there. I have a fresh set of clothes there," he added.

Kostas drove, Marika suggested it would be best to avoid I-95 in its entirety, so they used I-66 west to turn south on Route 29 to make their way through Culpeper, Virginia, then to I-64 east into Richmond.

As they entered the mostly rural byway, Route 29, Marika finally broke the silence, "I don't want to take it."

"Take what?" Kostas replied, knowing what she was referring to. He knew she was just as prone to changing the conversation during an uncomfortable subject as shifting gears back to it abruptly when she finally formulated her thoughts.

"The Promotion," she replied, annoyed at him for dragging it out of her this way. Then added, "Do you remember when you bought that old elliptical?"

He made a slight laugh, "Yeah, I do."

"And you remember how I got annoyed with you over the phone when you told me you bought it?" she asked.

He chuckled again, "Yeah, sure do. If I remember correctly, you slipped up prematurely, revealing your feelings for me. You asked me why I bought one when you already had one."

She punched him in the arm and said, "Exactly! I had already planned on you moving into my house at that time, so you could abandon the bachelor dungeon you called a home. I tipped my cards."

"I would like to think you tipping your cards was due to my superior interrogation skills, " he said, beaming in a mocking manner.

She punched him again, "Sta-ma-ta!" she added after the blow to his shoulder, telling him to cut it out in Greek.

Laughing, he said, "Never hit the driver!"

She began, "I wanted to tell you about the promotion and my decision not to take it. I want to retire in my own way and my own time."

"Why the cloak-and-dagger approach? I thought that was my shtick?" He replied, still with a bit of a laugh.

With an air of defeat lingering about her in the passenger seat, she said, "I want to retire, to do something else. Kostas, I want to be closer to you, I want what we always promised each other."

She took a deep breath. "I know you have responsibilities at MSGI; I have responsibilities to the Air Force. Something has to give for me to be able to see if this will ever be what we always said we wanted it to be. I decided it is the Air Force that will have to give, not my desire to be with you."

She exhaled deeply, as if a massive weight was now suddenly off her mind, and added, "Don't worry, I'll get my own place in Richmond, the Fan area has plenty of apartments and…"

Kostas cut her off, "Your turn to cut it out. You're moving in as soon as you're done up there."

She smiled and once again exhaled deeply.

Chapter 17

After parking the Subaru in the basement parking garage, Kostas and Marika made their way up to MGSI's office. Jess met them at the main entrance with a warm smile.

She hugged Marika and said, "So happy to see you!"

"How are Tess and the kids?"

"Fine, busy, and a handful. Almost as bad as taking care of this guy." Jess laughed with a jerk of her chin at Kostas.

He raised his hands in surrender, then said, "I'm not that bad!"

This time, changing the subject from him to elsewhere, he said, "Hey, Jess won another trophy for us here at MGSI."

"Did you?" Marika asked.

Jess blushed a bit and said, "Yes, I did."

Kostas added, "She took first place at the Smith Mountain Challenge. She beat out over two hundred of the country's top shooters, former and current military members, and civilians. She took out targets that ranged almost two thousand meters away."

"One more for the awards shelf! Congrats, Jess!" Marika said as she gave Jess a fist bump.

"It's a great stress relief." Jess shrugged. "Besides, I get to use all the fun toys in the MGSI armory, at Kostas's expense," she grinned.

"I just like knowing you can put three rounds in a teacup at over a thousand meters. May come in handy one day," he quipped.

As they passed Jess's office, Marika parted ways with Kostas with a sendoff of a wrinkled-up nose and a parting, "go shower, stinky boy," as she joined Jess in her office.

Kostas mock saluted her, then continued to his own office and private bathroom, complete with a shower and a change of clothes.

Chapter 18

After changing into a fresh set of clothes, he walked to his standup desk and monitors, then connected his laptop to the docking station. His phone buzzed, it was a text from Marika saying that she would pick him up at six tonight and that they WILL be going to dinner at Athena's Tavern tonight.

Guess I'm leaving the truck here tonight, he thought while smiling and replied with a yellow thumbs up emoji. As he swiped up with his thumb on the phone to lock the screen, he noticed the missed text from Wade that must have come in while he was in the shower. '???' was all it displayed on the screen.

He hit Wade's cell phone number and walked over to his office window. He heard a single ring, then it picked up. "God damn it, what the hell is going on? Why did you skip the FBI's brief last night?" came Wade's gruff voice from the other end of the line.

"Seemed like the smartest course of action once I saw an opening to egress the ambush that I was in," Kostas replied.

"What ambush?" Wade asked.

"Agent Hogan and her dossier on my whole career and personal life. It was like I was a direct suspect in the investigation. Did she ask you why I am on this investigation?" he replied.

"Yes, and I told her because of your subject matter knowledge of Program Paratiro and you're a proven damn good investigator in your own right. She mentioned nothing of the rest of your career and personal life," Wade replied.

"Well, I think if she could have shackled me to the table and put a polygraph on me, she would have. I think she would have waterboarded me if you didn't walk in." Kostas added.

"I don't understand. Why?" Wade said.

Kostas replied, "That's what I keep asking myself." He paused, "Was there anything useful in the brief? Any updates?"

"Yes, the FBI narrowed down the accelerant used in the truck fires to a combination of magnesium shavings and other elements. When the responding fire departments tried to extinguish the fires, the flames burned brighter when water was applied."

Nodding, Kostas said, "I do remember that the flames turn a bright blue and green when water hits burning magnesium."

"That's correct. Water is more fuel at over five thousand degrees Fahrenheit due to its oxygen content. Finally, they ended up using aircraft foam to put out the flames at both locations."

He paused, then continued, "The FBI also tracked down all the members of Paratiro. Erik Sharps is still living in Colorado after his separation from the Navy. He's a contracting officer with the Defense Contract Management Agency, has a low-key life with his family, and likes playing golf and attending Avs games." Referring to the National Hockey League's Colorado Avalanche.

"Scott Zillinski passed away at age forty-two at his home just outside Santa Fe, New Mexico. He was in home hospice, with blood cancer. Formerly, he worked at Sandia Labs after his Army separation.

After retiring from the Marine Corps, Jesse Wilson is now at Battelle Laboratories as the Chief of Defense Systems Development, Chem-Bio. No known connections to any domestic or foreign groups that would raise any flags. His Top Secret clearance with polygraph was just renewed four months ago. If there was a threat affiliation, we would likely have found it then.

Stephanie Turner, as you know, is now the Governor of Maine. She left the Department of the Navy and was voted in as a small town mayor in her hometown, where she grew up in Maine. She rapidly rose in the Democratic Party as their next high riser. No threat affiliations found with Stephanie."

He paused, then he continued, "Robert Chilcott, well, you know where Bobby is." Wade finished.

Robert Chilcott, or "Bobby," was a close friend of Kostas back in his DTRA days. Bobby was the only other Air Force officer detailed to Program Paratiro and from day one, that gave them a bond in the purple group of Army green, Air Force blue, Navy white, and Marine Corps red.

Kostas was with him three weeks before he finally succumbed to the cancer at the ripe old age of thirty-five. Over six years, Bobby had been hospitalized too many times to count; systematically having sections of his colon removed and chemotherapy treatments in a desperate effort to prolong his young life.

The timing of the final hospitalization happened to be the last week of Kostas's active duty service, and he out-processed the Air Force at Langley Air Force Base in Hampton, Virginia, only a short drive from where Bobby was in his final days. The two of them spent the day watching Netflix from his hospital room on a laptop and intermittently reminiscing on the old days—no tears, no regrets, just lighthearted banter and fondness for their past missions and drinking escapades. Bobby was always positive, right to the end.

Kostas remembered him saying, "Hey, I've got to drain the lizard, so if it smells like I'm pissing myself, well I am." Bobby said with a big smile, nodding to the colostomy bag hanging from the bed rail beside him.

Kostas's expression saddened but Bobby immediately kept his smile bright then said, "Hey man, at least were not getting shot at and pissing ourselves."

That was Bobby, always looking at what was going right and smiling. Then he added, "Hey, I'm going to make use of the drugs they gave me while I still can and see how many times I can get away with hitting this IV's trigger for the pain meds. Bastards won't let anyone bring in beer for me. I wish I could offer you some of this, but they ensured the IV only served one."

With that big smile, he added in a soft, sleepy voice, "Karen will be coming in tomorrow." Referring to his wife.

"I'll see you on the next mission" was the last thing Bobby said, and then he was asleep. That was the last time Kostas heard Bobby's voice. Three weeks later, Kostas found out he had passed.

"Did they discuss your file, Wade?" Kostas asked him, agitated.

"Yes, but it sounds like you got more of an information enema than I did," Wade replied to him with a concerned tone.

"That's an understatement. Hogan even brought Marika into it." Kostas said, then waited for a reply.

Wade asked, "What does she have to do with any of this?"

"I wish I had an answer for you, Wade, but I don't," he replied, then added, "Was there anything else the FBI found that is useful?"

"Somewhat, I'll know more later today. But they think they found this "Andy" that you relayed to me after interviewing Rizzarreo's widow, I'll keep you posted. For now, stay away from Hogan until we see what game she and the FBI are up to."

Wade paused for several seconds, then added, "Do you think it's all wrapped up in my office taking the lead on the investigation?" His voice seemed to be almost pondering the question himself while simultaneously asking Kostas.

"I thought of that, maybe, but I'm not sure." He replied to Wade.

"I'll keep you up to date on the FBI. What are you going to do next?"

"I have some research to do, I'm pulling in some quiet favors to see if I can flush out some theories I have," Kostas informed Wade.

"All right, circle back by 1300 tomorrow if not sooner," Wade said.

"Copy," Kostas replied, then hung up the phone.

Chapter 19

Kostas walked over to his desk and used his computer's instant messaging app to see if Jess had heard back from JP. The IM came back almost instantly, "I have coffee scheduled with both tomorrow, near their place at the Boathouse. Their two daughters want to know when Uncle Kostas is going to visit."

He replied to Jess with just a typed "TY," ignoring that last part of the message, painfully knowing and being reminded that he doesn't spend enough time with those who are close to him. He returned to the smart board that was strategically turned away from any window to block attempted surveillance from outside onlookers. He hit the remote to close the specially designed window curtains that prevented all forms of electronic surveillance, then waited for a few seconds for the lights in his office to turn on automatically.

Picking up the appropriate digital marker for the color black, he added thoughts and facts under several column headers that he had previously labeled at the top of the smart board before leaving for Belvoir.

The first column was labeled "Paratiro," the second, "I-95," and next to that, "I-64." He added three more to the board: "Leads, Action Items," and finally "Notes." Under the header of Paratiro, he already had listed every name that Wade had previously covered that was associated with the program, except for his own and Wade's. He added both.

Swapping the green marker for red, he made connecting lines on the digital board to the facts listed under the headers for both I-95 and I-64 scenes. Connecting the inputs under the columns for .556 and .223- headstamps, white box truck, evidence destroyed by fire, and so on.

Under the leads column, he updated the facts with what he learned from Rizzarreo's widow, Cabela's/Andy, and a W for Whittaker. Then, he placed an asterisk next to the name Andy and just below that, he added, MGSI/Kostas inquires with three question marks.

Was that a Lead or a Note? He contemplated for a moment, then decided to stick with his intuition and left it under leads.

He thought to himself, *hopefully tomorrow Jess will have some additional information after her coffee with JP to help him qualify if it was anything to consider at all.*

Then, under Action Items, he added, Jess = JP, then under that, Wade = Andy/FBI.

He took a step back and studied the information on the board. Feeling he missed something, he took a drink of water, returned to the board, and added 'Hogan???' to the Action Items column.

He glanced at his phone, which started to vibrate with a text message. He unlocked it and read, 'Call me—WM.'

He had just spoken with Wade less than three hours ago. It must be important, he thought, and dialed Wade's phone.

Wade picked up on the first ring, "You still at your office?"

"Yes," Kostas answered.

"Good, is your SCIF available?"

"Always."

"Get in there and access the encrypted link that is being sent via JWICS," or Joint Worldwide Intelligence Communications System, then General Wade Morris was gone.

Chapter 20

Kostas had Jess and the MGSI's security officer verify that all required security protocols were in place before logging into JWICS. Once he was alone in the room and Jess had changed the green light outside and inside the room to red, signifying sensitive or classified communications were taking place, Kostas logged in.

A live feed with a split screen emerged on the large display monitor mounted to the wall. One-half of the screen was divided into smaller boxes, showing Wade, the Director of the FBI, Jackson Dilbert, Jim from DIA, and several other individuals from various agencies, all on camera from either their desks or conference room tables. The other half of the display screen showed camera feeds from vehicle dashboards and integrated body cams.

Kostas heard Hogan's voice come through one of the vehicle's audio feeds, "Approximately five minutes away from takedown target."

Shit, Kostas thought to himself, who are they raiding? He couldn't text Wade for context on this last minute invite while in the SCIF; his phone was in the locker on the other side of the door. He would just have to ride it out.

"Three minutes out," Hogan's voice again.

Kostas now knew the feeling of impending dread and anticipation of being on this side of a raid, an observer. He had previously been one of the individuals who were wearing the integrated cameras—back then, they were on his helmet. This new experience from this side of the screen was not a welcome one. Minutes in silence passed, with only the hum of the SUV on the road accelerating, then her voice again, "Two out."

Drone imagery was added to the boxes on the screen, flickering at first, then clearing. The drone showed a large brown brick home with what looked like a multi-level deck attached to the rear of the home. The house had a long concrete driveway that passed through a small buffer of trees at the end of a cul-de-sac. Behind the large home was a dyed turquoise green pond with what looked to be a swim platform floating a small distance from a small sandy beach area. This was not an average person, or persons targeted for this raid, this was someone with money and likely power.

"Thirty seconds from target." Hogan's voice updated everyone. A second drone screen appeared; this one zoomed in closer to cover all exterior egress points of the targeted home. The bottom of the first drone's screen showed two armored black transport vehicles approaching the cul-de-sac from the south at a high rate of speed, the top of the imagery showed four black dots approaching from the north through what looked to be a fallow crop field surrounded by heavy woods, Kostas recognized the black dots as Light Strike Vehicles or LSVs, typically used by special forces teams in a multitude of terrains. The LSVs and armored vehicles were closing the gap between them and the house at a rapid pace.

"Teams Zulu and x-ray advance," again came Hogan's voice through the room's speakers.

On cue, two teams simultaneously emerged from the trees west and east of the house, the eastern team ready to breach the four-car garage. The team from the west took cover with shooting positions behind heavy equipment adjacent to a metal building near the home. As the LSV teams exited their vehicles, several took up positions to cover the breach teams as they made their way to the home.

Six individuals climbed the deck's stairs, and six others disappeared underneath the deck, presumably to breach a walkout basement door. The armored vehicle teams were also already out of the vehicles and assumed a mix of cover and breach positions near the front door. Again, Hogan's voice, "In three-two-one-BREACH!"

Kostas watched as the teams entered the house simultaneously and in concert through the front and rear doors. Kostas noticed a Whittaker for President flag displayed at the front door as one of the body cams walked to the door.

He noted that Hogan was the lead of the front door team. As she turned a corner, she was now clearly in an eat-in kitchen area at the rear of the home. As Kostas watched in anticipation, her bodycam displayed a man in a black Boonie-style hat and black T-shirt sitting behind a kitchen island.

Then, her bodycam went offline. Next, the screams of "GUN" and multiple rounds being fired made it impossible to understand any other words spoken by anyone.

All the other body cams seemed to be working, but the sudden and jerky movements of chaos during a firefight left little to be understood about what was actually going on. The gunfire stopped, then Hogan's voice was picked up from a team member's mic, "Suspect down, we need the medics, kitchen clear, report."

Next was a series of check-ins from all the other teams, pronouncing their areas of responsibility clear. As one of the breach team members walked through the dining room area to the kitchen Kostas watched the imagery from his bodycam and noticed that the man that had been sitting behind the kitchen island only moments ago was in no need of a medic, his face obliterated by several rounds entering and then exiting his head. In the camera view that Kostas had, no weapon was visible on the floor near the body.

As the live feeds were being taken down now that the show was over, Kostas quickly jotted down the coordinates that one of the drone screens displayed, showing its position. He punched them into the SCIF's laptop, the results were an area of a small township in the southern part of Michigan, Attica, Michigan.

The Google Maps-like satellite image displayed showed the large brick home, driveway, and dyed green pond. The audio came to life again, but with no video feed, the FBI Director thanked the team and gave them a "one hell of a good job!" and a "Thank you, Agent Hogan, excellent execution."

Kostas wondered if the director was speaking about the raid or the planned execution of Andy.

Wade's camera went dark and displayed "The participant has exited the meeting " in what used to be his display box on the monitor. The secure communications app on Kostas's laptop started to ring for an incoming call—it was Wade. Before answering the call, Kostas made sure he was fully logged out of the conference call, then hit accept with a click of his mouse.

The app was designed by Kosta's close friend Marten Raleigh, a brilliant software engineer and entrepreneur, to add an extra layer of protection to secure and encrypted text or calls on any device it was loaded to.

Marten had developed a post-quantum cryptography encryption key that significantly improved and remedied the vulnerabilities that other encryption standards like AES, RSA, and ECC failed to fix. The app was similar to Signal and WhatsApp, but it was now owned by the DoD with a code base secured in a DoD-approved cloud environment in a data center on US soil. It gave the user the ability to start at 2808-bit encryption, which already surpassed all other standards to 7893 bits.

Years prior, the Air Force gave Marten a grant to further the development of his invention to enhance it to unlimited bit encryption through the Small Business Innovation Research or SBIR program.

Soon after he delivered the operational prototype to the Air Force, it was promoted DoD-wide throughout the intel community.

It made Marten a wealthy man, and now he spends his time traveling to Arsenal FC matches with his son and returns to Richmond in the off-season. Kostas required his entire staff at MGSI to use the mil-spec version on their phones and laptops as a matter of corporate policy; he even loaded it onto Marika's phone.

"Sorry, I had no time to read you in prior to the raid. I found out at the last minute that you were not part of the loop," said the voice from Wade's image in his Belvoir office.

"Can you catch me up?" asked Kostas.

"The FBI tracked down your lead on 'Andy,' retired Air Force Colonel Andrew Kenna. Just as Rizzarreo's widow said, he lost his promotion to brigadier general and was forced to retire. He was found to be involved in a cover up that involved making some poor Airman the scapegoat for something that was a leadership failure on his part. He should have faced a court-martial; he was lucky. He has also been known to associate with militias and anti-government extremists. He owns a small construction company and has been hosting Whittaker fundraising events over the last several months. His wife divorced him several years ago, and his kids are all grown and estranged from him. Obviously, after what you just tuned in to, now deceased."

"Anything else?" Kostas asked.

"No, not at this time," came the response.

Kostas logged off and returned to his office. After another drink of water, he stepped back to the smart board, picked up the red marker, drew a line through Andy, and circled Hogan's name.

Chapter 21

He used the desk phone in his office to dial Wade's cell this time. "Did anything strike you as odd, Wade?" asked Kostas.

"Other than cutting part of my team out of the planning and execution of the raid? I was pissed, but that asshole Dilbert, fucking FBI Director, my ass! He said it was imperative that they move fast. None of this was even in Hogan's brief last night. Hell, they didn't even call me until after I last spoke with you this morning," snorted Wade.

"That is disturbing enough, but the fact that it had to take a considerable amount of time to organize a raid that size, they had to know who Andy was last night. No way that takedown was planned in a couple of hours, Wade. The logistics alone of getting all those assets in the local area take considerable time. On top of that, add Hogan's bodycam going offline when it did and a dead suspect." Kostas replied.

"Technical glitches happen all the time, you remember that. Those bodycams and helmet cams are always screwing up." dismissed Wade.

"I'm not sure; ten, fifteen years ago, yes, but now? Too many recent improvements have been made to those cameras, mainly for liability reasons. Now that our only solid lead is dead, I want to know who fired the shots at the suspect, and where is the 'gun' that the suspect supposedly had. I want to get my hands on Hogan's body camera." Kostas said in frustration.

"Wait a minute, Alpha. An after-action report is one thing; with those requests, you're basically calling the FBI dirty," Wade replied with apprehension.

"Maybe I am Wade. Something doesn't seem right with every nuance behind an FBI badge with this investigation. Hell, you're leading this effort, and they cut you out of this investigation and out of the best chance we had of catching these assholes." Kostas barked back at Wade.

Wade sighed, then began, "It's not that I don't see your point Kostas, it's just— shit— we have to go about this a different way to find out if there is anything there at all. It maybe a pissing contest simply due to my office leading the investigation."

"I don't disagree, Wade— yet. But hear me out."

"Go on."

For the next hour, Kostas laid out his strategy with General Morris, outlining how he wanted to approach the investigation moving forward. Before they both hung up, Wade agreed to the strategy, promised resources to Kostas, and held up his part of the plan.

Chapter 22

One of the burner phones located in the top right drawer of the desk buzzed. Only one person called on that particular phone; the recipient picked up. "Yes?"

"We have a problem." The caller relayed. "Additional forces are being deployed to the Lake Anna target site and others."

"Do they know?" asked the recipient of the call with concern.

"Not sure, it's historically a well-documented training event jointly between the Department of Energy and DTRA. At least, that is what they are calling it, training. It may have been moved up on the calendar as a precaution due to our phase one attacks on the interstates."

"Did they get anything out of Andy?" asked the recipient.

"No, that was ensured as soon as he became a liability," replied the caller.

"Is there any way to tie him back to phase one or the participants?" asked the recipient, this time with more of a worried tone than novel concern.

He paused, "Other than the uncorroborated claim that our deceased brother in arms made contact with Andy?" He added.

"No, I ensured that risk and liability were mitigated with all our soldiers during the phase one planning. His gear, weapon, and clothing were in the box truck with everyone else's. The magnesium shavings burned so hot that the FBI and ATF didn't even know that the equipment and ammunition from the attacks were even in the trucks when they burned. They will probably never figure that out. Nothing was left at either scene except the remnants of engine blocks and a molten mess." Replied the caller, projecting an air of smug confidence through the line.

"And the poor widow of our fallen brethren who sacrificed himself in battle on OUR behalf?"

The caller replied, "She has been well compensated for her recent actions." The reply came in a cold, dead tone.

"Good, and everyone else's status?" the recipient asked.

"Awaiting phase two instructions."

"Let's see how this joint training event with DOE and DTRA pans out. Tell the others to stand down and stand by for now, and continue their training and drills. God bless OUR Nation."

The caller's voice repeated, "God bless OUR Nation."

Both parties hung up, and then the digital recording stopped.

Chapter 24

Jess looked down at her phone on her desk as the screen lit up. As a text came in, she unlocked the screen. It was JP. "Hey Jess, do you know if Donner is CONUS or in Tel Aviv?"

She sent a text back, "Call me?"
She picked up on the first ring. It was JP's voice. "Hey Jess, how are Tess and the kids?"

"Great, other than when things are batt-shit crazy with all our schedules. You and the girls?"

"Same on the schedule front here, soccer, school, and everything else!" He laughed. "Hey, I would like to get Donner to give you a license for the new software that his company in Israel developed to confirm some of the legwork I did on the VIOP calls and data pull requests."

"Sure, I can call him on Kostas's behalf, but why not you?"

"I am working this off the books for you guys, the request can't come from me or DIA."

"I see, what do I ask him for?"

"Just say I need the crawl back to source tool, he'll know what you're asking for. I can confirm my findings once you get the link and license key from him."

"You got it, JP. Tell the girls I said hi, and we'll get the kids together soon."

"Sounds good, Jess." He clicked off.

Chapter 25

Kostas' cell buzzed; it was a call from Marika. He looked at the time before he answered it; it was a quarter to six. "On my way to pick you up," she said before Kostas could say a word. He smiled and started logging off all the electronics in his office.

As he started into the hallway to the elevator, his phone buzzed again. Wade's voice came right to the point, "No need for a wellness checkup on Rizzarreo's widow or daughter, both of their bodies were found by the local volunteer fire department in the burned-out remains of the singlewide trailer."

Wade paused, then said, "I'm coming more to your side of the estimation on what we are up against, Kostas." Then he hung up.

Kostas couldn't help but feel a pang of sorrow for the widow of Rizzarreo and the little girl, especially for the little girl. They were noncombatants in a world filled with chaos and combatants who did not care who got hurt, as long as their extreme ideologies and objectives tied to those ideologies were fulfilled.

Kostas wondered if Rizzarreo would have taken his life as he did on I-95 to protect the people behind the attack, knowing that this fate would fall to his wife and the little girl.

As Kostas walked through the revolving door at the front of the office building, Marika's red SUV was waiting on Tredegar Street.

She rolled down the window and asked, "Going my way?"

Kostas forced a smile, not letting the news that Wade had just conveyed to him moments ago ruin the next few hours. "Only if you're buying."

He got in. "Not a chance!" she replied as he closed the passenger side door. "Park at your place and walk over to A.T.?" she asked, referring to a local Greek restaurant, Athena's Tavern, just a short walk from his house in the Fan District.

"Sure, it's a beautiful evening out," he replied.

As they drove up the driveway, Marika parked her car past the second entry gate on a small, paved area next to Kostas's garage. They grabbed their belongings and made their way into the house through the back door. Kostas placed his backpack and weapons into a built-in steel wall safe that was flush against the mudroom wall, lightly concealed behind coats and jackets that were hung in front of it. Marika placed her small backpack, which she used as a purse and laptop carrier, on the bench. "I won't be needing that, you're paying," she said with a big triumphant grin.

"You might want to bring your ID if you want wine; you're a lot younger than me," he replied, emphasizing "a lot" with a wink, and then was rewarded with her patented right-handed slaps on his arm.

"Mr. Funny Boy, you're not driving now! I can hit you all I want," she said as they laughed.

It was a short walk to the restaurant. They chatted about their plans to go to the lake together, then walked under the Santorini blue awning on Robinson Street. Kostas opened the big wooden door to let Marika in and tested the lock and doorknob. "Yep, still working. The guy who replaced these knew what he was doing."

Christina, the owner and an amazing chef, looked up from the table she was standing at. She placed an order of grilled octopus on it and said in an admonishing tone, "Nothing like applauding your own work, Kostas."

Then she came over and gave Marika a big hug.

"I guess I know who the priority is," he chuckled.

"Of course she is!" said Christina, giving him a teasing, disapproving sideways glance. Then she smiled, "Come here!" while releasing Marika and giving Kostas an equal welcome bear hug. "Come, come, take your normal table," she instructed.

They made their way up the small set of stairs to the upper seating area, which Christina used for overflow and as an impromptu office to do her bookkeeping when needed. It was the first table outside the kitchen staff door, which generally would not be a desired seat in any restaurant. That was not the case in a family-run Greek restaurant; it was the best seat in the house. It allowed Kostas to talk to Christina and her daughters as they went back and forth serving the restaurant's customers, not to mention satisfying his personality quirk of always wanting to monitor entrances and exits in public places.

"The normal dishes?" Christina asked.

Marika exclaimed, "Parakaló, kai efcharistó!" or please and thank you!

"What, I don't get a say-so?" Kostas teased.

Marika smiled and looked directly at Christina and simply said to him, "όχι." or no in Greek. "You can eat here anytime; I haven't been here in ages."

Christina laughed then asked her daughter Georgetta who was behind the bar to get a carafe of their favorite Greek dry red wine and two glasses.

Pleadingly, Marika asked Christina, "Please tell me you have it tonight?"

She smiled, "Of course, Kostas sent me a text this morning. Tonight's off menu dessert is portokalopita!" Christina proclaimed with beaming pride. "I just took it out of the oven a few hours ago, luckily I had all the ingredients on hand." She was referring to the classic Greek syrup-soaked dessert made with phyllo dough and with a rich orange flavor.

Marika visibly melted into the booth with a huge smile.

The three of them spent the next two hours catching up and eating several traditional small plates of food, grilled octopus, saganaki, and melitzanosalata, an olive oil and eggplant dip with garlic, lots of garlic. Kostas added an order of Christina's homemade pastitsio, which one portion could feed three hungry people. Marika took a few bites just before Kostas finished the whole plate of the Greeks' version of lasagna. After sharing the portokalopita between the two of them with two small forks, both Marika and Kostas said goodbye to Christina and her daughters, then started walking back to Kostas's house.

"Jess says you're really slammed with this investigation." Marika broke the silence as they turned the corner onto Monument Avenue.

"Yeah, I'm sure you can imagine. Hey, you know I can't..." he tried to finish, but she cut him off.

"I know you can't talk about it. I've been around your career a long time, Kostas. I was simply saying thank you for making the time tonight," she said with a smile, locked her arm inside of his, and gave it a squeeze with both her arms and body. "And thank you for what you said in the car on the way down from Belvoir, I didn't mean to put you on the spot for a place to move into. I can still find my own place once I retire."

They continued for three more steps, then Kostas stopped and turned to her, bringing her close and looking into her eyes.
He began, "I have lived a lot of lives. Some of them were glimpses of amazing things, some of them are scars on my sole to this day, you have been the majority of the amazing Marika." then kissed her.
"You're moving in." he whispered after the kiss, then with a smile he asked, "Do I have work to do tonight?"

She smiled and then whispered, "you bet you do." Then she regained her purchase on his arm, squeezed it again and then led him back the rest of the way down Monument Avenue.

Chapter 26

Kostas's phone vibrated on the charger placed on the nightstand next to the bed. It was a quarter past four in the morning. He quickly picked it up from the charger in hopes of not disturbing Marika's sleep, walked naked out into the attached den of the master bedroom, and closed the door.

"Yes?" he asked the unknown caller with a Northern Virginia area code.

"Kostas, this is Hogan. 'Eh, Katheryn… Katheryn Hogan."

"Agent Hogan, it's a little early, and I would prefer you go through General Morris's office to make contact with me."

"I apologize, and I figured you were an early riser. I think we got off on the wrong foot, we are on the same team after all." Hogan said into the phone.

Kostas didn't reply. There was a long pause, then, "Let's meet for lunch and start again. I'll be in the Richmond FBI Field Office today for a 9:00 a.m. brief. I'm on my way down now. What do you say? Let me pick the tab up as a peace offering. Say at 1:00 p.m." Again, there was a long pause that forced Hogan to ask, "Kostas, are you still there?"

"Yes, I'll text this number the location to meet at 1:00. Which office?"

"' Eh, what?"

"Which office is your brief? Parham Road or Greencourt Road?" he asked.

"Oh, the Parham Road Office." She replied.

"Ok, I'll text you a location that is relatively close to there." He then hung up and dialed Wade's number.

Chapter 26

It was after 6:00 a.m., and Marika made her way downstairs and into the kitchen.

Kostas was standing behind the island counter with nothing but his underwear on pouring coffee from the French press into two mugs. "I timed it exactly right, so I don't have to do any work." Marika joked. "And I see your pajamas haven't changed." teasing him as she looked him up and down while walking over to him. She stood up on her tip toes and kissed him, "Good morning."

With a smile, he replied, "Kaliméra." or good morning. "If my memory serves me correct, I've been doing most of the work the last couple of nights." he added with a big toothy grin.

That quip again earned him a number of slaps on his arm as she bit her lower lip as she could only do while trying to suppress a smile.

They sat on the couch together and started watching the morning news on CBS 6.

"I always enjoy watching Tom do the weather in the morning, it's not the same in Northern Virginia." said Marika after sipping her coffee.

"The weather? he said teasing her, "Should I be jealous of Tom?" Kostas asked with an eyebrow raised.

"The feel of the city, how it's conveyed on the local news. I like it better down here and no; he has the weather; you have my heart." she replied then blushed a bit.

"So does that mean I am back in the nice Greek boy category for your parents?"

"So far. You've racked up a few points." she smiled, then added, "Big day for you?"

"Too early to tell, maybe." regaining his stoic manner.

"I noticed you got up for a phone call this morning, Wade?"

"No, but I did call him after that early call. Hey, I will be bouncing around all over today, make yourself at home you have the keys to everything and…" He paused, "I'm glad you came down Marika." and smiled again.

"Me too, now go do what you have to and come back to me." she said with a beaming look about her.

Kostas came to mock attention and saluted her in his underwear then said, "Yes ma'am!" and sped off upstairs as she laughed and threw a balled-up napkin at him. As he ascended the stairs two at a time, he shouted down, "Trader Joe's frozen pizzas and wine tonight? Stay in?"

"It's a date!" Then she went back to the weather with Tom and her coffee.

Chapter 27

Kostas took an Uber to the office since his truck was still parked there. He passed Jess's office; she sat staring from the side of her monitor with a big grin. Kostas ignored the grin and asked her, "Don't you have someone to meet with this morning?"

"I already met with JP. You're kind of late. JP's girls want to know when Uncle Kostas and Aunt Marika are coming by."

He ignored the last part of the sentence. "Do you want me to come to your office for the debrief?" she finished.

"Sure, I need to get a cup of coffee first."

"Late night?" Jess asked with an even bigger grin below her searching blue eyes.

"Can we get back to work, Jess?"

"Sure, never mind, I will get my intel updates from Marika later."

"I don't doubt it," he said, defeated.

Kostas returned with his coffee and sat opposite Jess at the small conference table in his office. "JP verified there were no officially logged records of inquiries from the FBI or any other Government agency on you or MGSI. The phone numbers used to call the MGSI main corporate line were untraceable, likely burner phones or VoIP apps on a computer with Northern Virginia and DC numbers."

She paused, flipped the digital page on her tablet with her index finger, and continued. "JP did say that the intel community is jumping through their asses trying to run down a massive number of leads and tips that are flooding in about the attacks, which you can imagine. One was of particular interest to him. How he zeroed in on this one, I have no idea, but kudos to him!"

Kostas looked up from his coffee, raising both dark eyebrows behind the steam of the cup, seemingly asking, "Well?" without a word being said.

"It seemed like nothing at first, all other analysts missed it, but someone pulled a public query yesterday on MGSI's government and defense contracts and the associated government funding from Congress's contract spend tracking tool."

She flipped another page, "The same day, a concerned and anonymous citizen used North Anna Power Station's 1-800 information line for public inquiries. The caller asked why there was a buildup of troops at the facility about ten minutes after DTRA rolled through the gates at the nuclear power plant. The data pulled from Congress's spending tool was logged another ten minutes later. No one other than JP would have caught that; he said he only did because you had me alert him that something was up. He also asked me to pull a favor from Donner and get access to his new software so that he could validate his findings. JP feels confident it's accurate."

Kostas allowed a small smile behind his cup and said, "Good 'ol JP."

Changing the subject with a disapproving tone, she looked at him and said, "Did you really sneak up on his left side after he lost his eye, just to scare him?" Jess asked.

"He told me you used to do that— on purpose."

"Military gallows humor, he needed cheering up," he dismissed. "And?"

Still with a disapproving sisterly look, she continued, "JP found the number was a 540-area code with a Fredericksburg, Virginia exchange prefix. This would make it plausible that it was a resident outside North Anna Power Station or in the Lake Anna area."

"But? I sense a but coming." Kostas interjected.

"Nothing sneaks up on you, Kostas, unlike you did to poor JP," she reproved with a frown.

"Anyway, the call and the query were from the same IP address and from the same cellular hotspot. A virtual private network was used for the call and the data query. JP said they weren't too bright because the VPN wasn't bouncing all over the globe, concealing the location. While the precise location wasn't known, JP felt confident it was Northern Michigan, likely the Upper Peninsula, the Newberry area. Seems they got lazy, sloppy, or both with the parameters of the VPN's configuration."

She paused, "One more thing: the IP address and hotspot were also linked to the inquiries on MGSI's main phone line."

"So, what's the Intel Officer in you say?" Kostas asked.

"The caller was not in the 540-area code. They were likely in Michigan. This means there are other eyes on the ground that provide human intelligence from an observation post or from a need to know authority on the inside."

She took a sip of her coffee in quiet contemplation, then interjected, "One more possibility, the surveillance could be digital." Jess said in a confident tone.

"But whoever they are, they thought of checking our government contracts at MGSI to see if there were any new contracts or modifications to track the buildup or surge in our training support,"

Kostas asked, "And?"

"Which wouldn't give them any results at all. All our sensitive national security contracts are a legal exception to the requirements for posting to government portals or repositories that are not classified at the TS-SCI level." Referring to Top Secret and Sensitive Compartmented Information.

Kostas's grin widened, and he placed his now empty cup on the table.

She continued, "So, they have some intel assets, but no real understanding of how everything works." She paused to frown again, "It's like it was in the early days of Desert Shield and Desert Storm. Saddam knew Allied forces were being mobilized, but his war machine had no way of knowing how ours would be deployed in the area of operation or even what the Allies' real capabilities were. There was no real ability for counter-intel operations. Saddam's commanders were left to fill in the blanks and act independently on the ground as conditions dictated. Instead of as one complete force," she finished.

Kostas nodded, "Someone has taken the liberty to fill in the operational information gaps without the benefit of reliable and actionable intel."

Jess looked at him, deepening her frown. "This is not good, Kostas. This is an unpredictable foe, a rabid dog, running around biting anything that moves."

"That's exactly what I am hoping for, Jess," he replied as he rose from the table and gently fist-bumped Jess in a congratulations gesture.

Jess looked puzzled, "What's up your sleeve, Boss?"

Dismissing her question, he replied, "Well done, you, JP, and the team! Thank you!"

Kostas left his office to ask the company security officer to prepare the SCIF for an outgoing call.

The light inside the room turned red, and Kostas dialed the number.

Chapter 29

"Yes?" The voice on the other end said.

"Frank… It's Kostas."

"You old Malaka! Where have you been hiding?" Frank asked in a cheerful tone.

"In the Colonies, you old Limey," Kostas said sarcastically with a chuckle.

"I thought someone told me that, Virginia. Richmond, right?

Kostas replied, "That's right."

Kostas first met Frank Cromwell while deployed in the Middle East and assigned to a Joint Allied Operation focused on finding and combating WMD.

Cromwell, then a British Intelligence Officer, was short in stature, balding in his early thirties, and with a stereotypically pale complexion. He was now a career MI6 intelligence Agent.

Their first introduction came in a R&R coffee tent called Jack's on the base from which they were operating. A brew hang-out with all the free tea and coffee you could drink for the Allied forces stationed there.

Jack's had been constructed from a spare barny-style tent, similar to the tents immortalized on the television series MASH The 4077th's lookalike interior was hastily outfitted with bookshelves of cinder blocks and wood salvaged from old pallets and shipping materials. Books would come in from all over the world, paperbacks, hardcovers, and magazines, all donated in care packages or left behind by the people who rotated out, either to their respective home countries or other assignments within the AOR or area of responsibility. It had a rustic coffee shop vibe with even music playing from a donated speaker system.

The social area within the tent was complete with comfortable chairs that may have or may not have come from one of Saddam's palaces. However, there were mostly narrow standup tables in the middle of the tent where you would belly up to drink coffee or tea and initiate a conversation.

One day before his shift, Frank jokingly told Kostas over tea, a spot of tea for him and a mug of coffee for Kostas, that the military power of the US and its corresponding defense budget could overtake the UK in a single military operation with one Air National Guard unit when compared to Britain's corresponding war-making resources. They both had a good laugh over that, then became fast friends.

"How are you, old chap? Messy business that in Virginia, sorry about that."

"Yeah, a shit show on two main interstates, hundreds either dead or wounded. That's what I'm calling about. I need your help."

"Done, how can I be of service to you, Yanks?"

134

Kostas spent the next forty-five minutes updating Cromwell on the situation since the attacks were carried out and read him in at the level Wade had authorized him to, and then a little more than Wade authorized.

"Good to be working with you again, you old Malaka!" Cromwell said with cheer in his voice at the end of the conversation.

Kostas replied, "You Limeys ever going to give my ancestors back all those ancient artifacts you took from Greece?"

"Always a pleasure, old man! Now I have some things to take care of on your behalf; we need to get a pint soon!" he was gone.

Chapter 29

Kostas was sitting in the restaurant booth and had already surveyed the surrounding area as well as the inside of the restaurant, including the restrooms. At 12:50, he punched in the numbers that Hogan had called from into his phone. He texted her, "Mission BBQ, Broad Street and Glenside."

He didn't want to give her too much of a heads-up on the location just in case there was some more FBI leg-pissing going on. He wanted to control all potential variables in their meeting as best he could.

On the way to the restaurant, he called Wade and gave him as much of an update as he could. "Operation Limey Sparrow is a go."

"How long will it take to get the report back from Cromwell?" asked Wade.

"Twenty-four to forty-eight hours max."

"I hope it's on the sooner end of that range. I want to put this to bed one way or another."

Wade added. "You on your way to lunch?"

"Yes."

Wade said, "Call me back and let me know how the brisket is."

"WILCO."

A few moments later, Agent Hogan walked in. "I almost made it on time, sorry. Once you're in the office, it's hard to get out of it. I'm sure you can relate," she said to Kostas with a pleasant and disarming smile.

"How about we order?" she asked.

"FBI buying or you personally?" Kostas asked.

"Hmm, that didn't even occur to me, I'll keep it off the taxpayer's tab since it's not Bookbinders or Lemaire at The Jefferson," again with a well-practiced pleasant smile.

They walked up together to order. Kostas chose pulled pork and slaw, and Hogan chose baby back ribs and cut fries.

"I love ribs," she said as they sat back down.

"I prefer the pulled pork, Carolina style. Not much of a KC sauce guy." Referring to the Kansas City style of sweet BBQ sauce.

"Why... because you're already sweet enough?" she quipped, attempting to disarm or flirt with him.

"Something like that. Let's get to the point, Agent Hogan," he shot back in his deadpan tone.

She picked up a rib from her basket, twirled it around in her mouth sucking the meat entirely off in a slow methodical manner, demonstrating a skill that she seemed to want to convey to Kostas. "You can call me Katherine."

"Okay, Katherine."

"I do love ribs!" closing her eyes and gushing, then paused.

After making a show of swallowing deeply, she said, "I honestly think we got off on the wrong foot. As I said, we are on the same team. I was just taken aback by your inclusion in the investigation by General Morris, not because you're not qualified. Just that you were at one of the two scenes. Tensions were running high for all of us that day; I admittedly handled it poorly. I want to bury the hatchet, make it up to you."

"Make it up to me? It's not necessary. We can just move forward with the investigation. Lunch is enough to reboot it between us. We're both professionals."

Kostas allowed an awkward silence to hang in the air. Hogan said, "So, I hear your old unit at DTRA's WTSG is conducting some joint training exercises with DOE for counter terrorism operations. Is MGSI included?" Hogan asked innocently.

Kostas shrugged, "We've had the contract to support those training events for over three years. Nothing new. I don't get personally involved. All the MGSI employees are well qualified and capable of facilitating the training. I don't even remember the particular scope of work." He lied. "My chief operating officer keeps me informed at a high level,"

She smiled and selected another rib from the basket in an almost-eeny, meeny, miny, moe twirl of her right index finger. Then did her best to one up her previous technique on the first rib; grudgingly, Kostas had to admit, she succeeded.

"Well, you have certain talents and resources, and I have certain talents and resources. I thought we could team up together," she said, then wiped the sauce from the corner of her mouth with a paper napkin.

"We are teamed up, have been since I walked into the Dulles conference room for the first time with General Morris."

She held another rib close to her mouth and gently exhaled directly to it, then said, "I was thinking more of a direct one-on-one relationship. Like I said, I have talents and I am more than a bit curious about the ones I don't know about you already."

Then, with little effort, it seemed, the technique of the second rib was topped with the third.

Playing a long, he said, "Ok, what exactly did you have in mind?"

"Ever been to The Inn at Little Washington?" she asked seductively with that tilt of the head she demonstrated while interrogating him at Wade's office and with a not-so-innocent smile.

"A couple times, nice place with great food."

She smiled, "I was thinking we could continue the investigation from there for a couple of nights?" she replied without moving her head from the tilt. Kostas now noticed the smile turn impish.

He answered, "The food is good, but I think I'll have to take a raincheck until the investigation is concluded and those assholes are brought down."

Not seeing headway, she shifted tactics, her impish smile transformed into a momentary pout. "Come on, Kostas. The FBI has dozens of analysts combing over everything, not to mention DAI, DHS, ATF, and other resources. I'm sure you have your own MGSI people on it as well. We can get back to Belvoir if needed quicker from there than you can from Richmond. Who knows, a little break might be what we both need to solve this together."

He took the last forkful of his pulled pork, swallowed, and said, "Once I start something, I see it through without distractions."

He noticed the change in her demeanor and facial expressions. She went to a squinty-eyed, puzzled look, like she was trying to determine a seven-letter verb in a crossword puzzle for sex.

He continued, "But I thank you for the olive branch and the lunch." He did not mention the invitation to the three-star Michelin restaurant and inn.

He wiped his mouth, stood, and said, "We will have to do this again. I'll buy next time."

She looked at him and forced a smile, but did not stand.

"Running off so soon?"

"Like you said, I have my people working on this, too. I need to get a status update before the next task force meeting with General Morris."

He started to turn and walk away, then stopped and asked, "By the way, what happened to your bodycam during Andrew Kenna's takedown in Michigan?"

She shrugged her shoulders and said, "Don't know, those things fail all the time. I'm just glad it wasn't my weapon that failed."

"Yeah, I've heard that about those cameras. Extremely fortunate for you," and he walked out of the restaurant and made his way to his truck.

As Kostas pulled out of the parking lot onto Glenside, he turned to the right to see Jess's SUV parked in full surveillance mode at the back of the lot. Then, as he drove off, a text from Jess came in; all it displayed was a small yellow hand with a thumbs up.

Chapter 30

The sound of gunfire was constant. Rounds were fired from both fully automatic and single-shot weapons, a mix of handguns, assault weapons, and bolt-action long-distance rifles. The rate of fire had to be in the hundreds of rounds per minute. The day was overcast, but dry overall. The temperature was somewhere in the low fifties.

He stopped to survey all that was in front of him. He wondered to himself silently, *Will this be enough? Will they be ready? Hell, yes, it will!* he smiled.

The phone in his chest pocket vibrated. Red pulled himself away from his second-story window above the armory overlooking the shooting line on the range.

"Yeah?" he said into the phone after hitting the screen's green icon.

"How is Anna?" came the voice. Anna was an agreed upon code for the North Anna Nuclear Power Facility in central Virginia, over nine hundred miles and a fifteen-hour drive from where he was currently in the Upper Peninsula of Michigan.

"She is being monitored, and the test results should tell us more soon. From what you have told me previously, the local doctor feels confident in the upcoming procedure," Red replied.

"How about her relative in Tennessee? The donor information to help Anna's upcoming procedure?" Now the voice was referring to the Department of Energy's Oak Ridge National Laboratory,, or ORNL, in Tennessee.

"The procedure for the close relative is scheduled, and unless something has changed with the doctor, we are also optimistic."

"Good," said the voice on the other end of the phone. I cannot stress enough how important the first procedure is to the success of the second."

"The team is aware and takes your advice very seriously."

"As they should," the voice replied.

Red asked, "Has the doctor covered any potential new complications for either procedure?"

The voice replied, "Some, but she has plans to avoid or mitigate the risks of those complications."

Red asked, "Can we, as family members, help with any of that? We will do we can anything to help."

"You and the family's dedication and willingness to be there are noted and appreciated, but I have to agree with the doctor and her plan. Be patient, your time and the family's time will come soon." Then the phone was silent.

Red looked back out the window at the firing line and the range targets. He placed the phone on his desk, then paced back and forth the length of the office and thought to himself, there must be more we can do instead of just training up here. Things have not exactly gone as planned; we need to mix it up.

The I-95 operation was not without losses, and now that the Government has brought in that outside contractor, there are unforeseen complications. Our loss must be avenged.

Red picked up the phone and dialed the so-called doctor.

"Why are you calling me?" the woman asked after she picked up. The caller's name on her end of the conversation read only 'R' on the screen.

"Just a concerned family member who is offering to bring extra support before both procedures take place. Thought we could be helpful given new circumstances and issues." Red said in a light and eager tone.

"There are no issues or circumstances that cannot be managed here locally. Your support is not needed. Stick to the plan." Then she hung up.

"Fucking bitch, who does she think she is?" Red yelled as he kicked a chair across the room.

"Fucking bitch! Think she is smarter than me; I don't trust that bitch!"

Red opened the door from his office, then yelled, "Todd! Get in here now!"

Todd, a tall man in his early thirties, balding and dressed in a mismatched combination of multi-camo pants and a camo T-shirt, jumped to his feet and quickly made his way into the office. "Sir?"

"Todd, I don't like being out of the loop with information, that bitch down in Virginia can't be trusted, I know it. I never thought she could be trusted, ever since she came to me and Lawrence. She thinks she is the only one that has a need to know," he scoffed.

"She will fuck this opportunity up for us to make things right, I know it! Never trust a god damn woman!" Red practically screamed.

"I want you to find out all you can about this Papadopoulos and MGSI. Get a couple of our trusted family members that are already down there to dig around. Get me more information than that bitch is giving me."

Todd saluted and said, "yes, sir." Then he exited the office as quickly as he came in.

I need some range time, Red thought to himself with a smile, and headed downstairs after retrieving his AR-15 from the rack behind his desk.

Chapter 31

Kostas phoned Wade on the way back to the office. "How was the brisket?" Wade asked.

"Soaked in a honeypot," referring to the espionage or human intelligence strategy to gain sensitive information through a suggestive or sexual relationship.

"I don't recommend it. I went with the pulled pork."

"Carolina style?" Wade asked.

"Isn't that the only way?"

With his southern drawl Wade replied, "You're damn right it is! Honeypot, huh... really?"

"Even used the smoked ribs as a prop to illustrate her point."

"You don't say... that had to be entertaining," Wade replied.

"She was convincing."

"Jess on it?"

"Yep, I think Jess will enjoy this more than she probably should. I don't think Hogan is her type, and I know for a fact that she could see the 'rib-job' from her observation point. I had picked the table before Hogan arrived." Kostas added.

Wade chuckled, "I feel sorry for Hogan a bit now," continuing to laugh.

"Don't. Hey, anything on Lawrence or Red?"

"Yes, call me when you get back to the office, but do it from the SCIF. I have some files to share." Wade said as his laugh died down.

Chapter 32

Kostas checked with the FSO back at the office to make sure the SCIF was prepped and available. Then he sat and logged into the comms, Wade answered.

"You got the files?" Wade asked.

"I just pulled them up. The first is Lawrence Johnson's." Kostas looked at the pictures in the file on the screen.

First, a Vietnam Era photo of an Air Force Airman in the standard-issued OG-107 uniform, commonly known back then as fatigues. Then, there was a Michigan driver's license picture from 1998, and then a notably aged, weathered face. A man quickly approaching his eighties with a gray mullet and matching mustache.

Wade began an overview of the file, "Lawrence Anthony Johnson, Vietnam Vet, Air Force. Munitions Systems Specialist, separated as an E4 Buck Sergeant. He worked mostly on the bombs and other ordnance that were dropped in North Vietnam. He knows how to put them together and take them apart. Owns a concrete company that provides mostly commercial flat work and some residential in the DMV area." Referring to the acronym commonly used for the DC, Maryland, and Virginia area.

He continued, "A lot of subcontracts for work with Andrew Kenna's construction company. Odd since Kenna's company primarily worked in Michigan and Johnson's in the DMV."

"Know the addresses?" Kostas asked.

"Besides the DMV home and business address, there is a limited liability corporation that happened to be in his name; and get this, a Joel Johnson, his younger brother, Red. You'll see in his file that at one time he had red hair, now turned white."

Kostas clicked to the next set of photos.

"So, we now know Red and Lawrence." Kostas interrupted.

"Seems so, the LLC has a PO Box in Newberry, a small town in the Upper Peninsula of Michigan. The LLC is listed as the owner of three hundred and twenty acres of undeveloped land adjacent to the Newberry State Forest. Tax records show no structures on the land. Satellite imagery tells a different story; it is definitely developed with several livable buildings and storage sheds."

Kostas interrupted, "Any signs of training areas or ranges?"

"Oh yeah, two long-distance ranges, one up to three hundred meters, the other close to a thousand meters and a pistol range. We were able to zoom in to see that some of the heavy earth-moving equipment near the ranges had Kenna's construction company's logo on them. Also, the latest pass shows a rope course and running trails throughout the property, according to the analysts. A twelve-foot chain-link fence surrounds the entire three hundred and twenty acres, with some concertina wire. The intel analysts also estimate living quarters for up to two hundred and fifty personnel. Thermal imaging has determined that there are only seventy at most currently occupying the site."

"Asshole membership down?"

Wade answered, "More like build it and they will come, I think."

"And Red? Any nice to knows there?" Kostas asked.

"Never served in the armed forces, but he dressed like he did in the seventies. More of a want to be. He was too young to serve during the Vietnam War like his brother. He was still in high school. In the early nineties, he got picked up by a small township in lower Michigan as a deputy sheriff. He volunteered for SWAT training and became a team sniper. No documented opportunities to use the skill set in his official record."

"All right, I'll comb through these files and get a few of my analysts on them also. Might be able to add a few more pieces to the puzzle. Can we maintain the satellite passes?"

"Way ahead of you, I already ordered all orbiting assets to perform a full scope until otherwise ordered by me only. I kept the order TS-SCI. No one outside of the DoD will be able to access the order, not even the FBI," Wade said with a self-appreciative tone.

"Good, I'll check back today if I or my team finds anything else."

"Before you go, has Jess checked in?" Wade asked.

"Yes, but just with the predetermined code sequences for 'I'm still alive and on the job."

"You sure I can't get her back in uniform? I…"
Kostas cut him off, "I told you, don't even think about it."

Wade chuckled, "Yeah, I know, I just miss well-experienced battle-hardened operators."

"We're not operators." Then he clicked off.

Chapter 33

Hogan grabbed her phone and punched in the number; it was picked up immediately. "Is your guy up north going to be a problem?"

"I don't know what you mean," said the man's voice on the other end.

Exasperated, Hogan replied, "I'll be in your office within the hour, and I'll explain."

She punched in another number, this time a text, "I potentially have a job for you. You're availability?"

As she drove in silence, her phone beeped and vibrated. The incoming text read, "Currently available, inquiry to follow. – KV"

Chapter 34

Kostas was grateful that the evening went by uneventfully. He and Marika had a quiet evening eating Trader Joe's mushroom pizzas and sharing a bottle of Sauvignon Blanc from his private cellar.

They woke and repeated the morning coffee ritual, then Kostas went downstairs for a swim.

When he got out of the shower, Marika was lying on the bed, going through emails on her phone. "Work?" he asked.

"A little bit of that, a little bit of updating my mom. She says hello, and she wanted me to tell you that it would be nice if you were her favorite son-in-law."

"Since your only sibling is your brother, and he is into women, I would say I would be her only son-in-law. It kind of dilutes the honor," he teased, then added, "So, I am back on the 'Nice Greek Boy' list?"

"Don't get cocky." she quipped with a smile, then added, "I'm going to have to get back to Belvoir tomorrow afternoon."

"So soon? I was just getting used to you being around again."

"Duty calls, " she said, rolling over and sitting at the end of the bed. "Sound familiar?"

Kostas sat next to her, then said, "OUCH! That was a low blow. Hey, I'm going to meet Marten over at Nick's at ten this morning. There is an Arsenal match, and we have a few things to catch up on, then I'm going to swing back by to get the truck and head to the office."

"I'll be here. I'm going to go downstairs and exercise. It's convenient having a private gym in the basement," she said, then added, "He's back in Richmond?"

"Unfortunately, yes, his cancer. He has a procedure coming up at VCU's Massey Cancer Center."

"Oh my god, I thought he was in remission."

"So did he."

She looked immediately sad and said, "Please tell him I said hello."

"I will. We can talk when I get back about dinner. If Jess is back in town, how about we take her and Tess out tonight, and they can get a sitter?"

Her somber look from the news about Marten faded, and she said, "That's a great idea! I'll set it up."

"I'll see you around halftime."

"Have fun." Then she kissed him.

Chapter 35

Kostas grabbed his holsters, then a light jacket, and made his way out of the front of the house for the short walk to Nick's on the corner of Mulberry and Broad.

Nick's Bar and Grill was the home of the Richmond Gooners Club, the local group of dedicated fans that intensely supported the North London English Premier League Team Arsenal. 'Intensely' may be an understatement.

The official nickname of the Arsenal Football Club is The Gunners; however, the fans had proudly adopted the name Gooners largely due to one of Arsenal's so-called firms being called the Goon Squad. A name which is said to have merged with the club nickname over time to form "Gooners." Marten was one of those proud Richmond Gooners.

Arsenal was up one—nil early in the first half. It may have been just after ten in the morning, but Marten and Kostas had two pints of Guinness in front of them. It was a Gooners game after all.

They both waited for the two stouts to go from a golden tan to solid black with a thin line of tan foam at the rim, then clinked the pints together and drank deeply.

"What's the prognosis?" asked Kostas.

"Not bad, but not great."

"How is Shane taking it?" asking about Marten's only son.

Shaking his head back and forth after he took another sip of his pint, Marten said, "He is a great kid, ha! Kid… he is almost nineteen now. It's not like he hasn't been through this with me before."

Then he paused, "The doctor said a few rounds of chemo after the surgery. You know… I can kick myself for not taking all of this more seriously twenty years ago. First a few spots on my arms, then the one on my forehead, and now in my chest." Laughing he added, "it's not the luck of the Irish that's for sure. The curse of the Irish American skin more like."

He took another sip of his Guinness, "How many of us with some form of cancer does that make?

"Too many."

"Yeah, too many of us. The bombs and bullets weren't the real hazards, at least not for us." Marten laughed grimly.

"Doc carved another divot into the middle of my back last year; the biopsy came back positive, but she thinks she got it all." Kostas immediately regretted his comment.

To trade tit for tat with someone who has been through the wringer that Marten had, was not a fair comparison.

He quickly added, "Sorry, I know that doesn't compare to what you have been through, Marten. Or any of the others."

The bar erupted with cheers, two-nil Arsenal over Chelsea.

Then Kostas added, "Hey, Marika says hello and asks about Shane. She's at the house. Do you want to pop over at the half and say hello?"

Marten's spirit seemed to improve, "Absolutely!" he exclaimed then continued, "The Gooners have this in the bag, Chelsea is absolute shite this year. One more before the road?"

"Not me, thanks. I'll take water, no ice. Still have a lot of work to do today." Kostas said.

Marten finished his new pint with a well-practiced single tilt of the glass that would make a college frat boy look at him in awe.

Kostas paid the tab, and they walked out and turned onto Mulberry then headed south toward Monument.

As they passed the alley behind the bar, Kostas looked to his right and then instinctively left to check for traffic coming down the alley. He noted a Michigan State license plate and a Detroit Lions bumper sticker attached to a blue Chevrolet pickup truck parked in the lot adjacent to a bank across the street.

Kostas stopped and knelt to check his boot laces, which he already knew did not need to be tightened or retied. He used this opportunity to observe the two men in the truck.

Marten took one more step then turned and looked down at him, "Still wearing those Docs?" he said with a smile.

Kostas rose, slapped him on the shoulder, and whispered, with a smile and a whisper, "Can you run?"

"Not fucking likely." Marten replied and then added forebodingly, "I know that look on your face and I never liked it."

"Can you fight?" Kostas asked.

"I can cause some interference, maybe get lucky."

"Ok, just stay clear of my shooting lanes and let cancer kill you not these fucks. I take it you can still shoot."

Marten replied with a wide grin that split his graying mustache and beard and a single nod.

Just then, Kostas heard the truck's two doors close.

Chapter 36

One block away from Kostas and Marten, near the corner of Arthur Ashe and Grace Street, a young brunette woman in her mid-thirties exited her apartment, stepped out onto the sidewalk, and turned the corner onto Grace.

She was taking a midday break from her normal remote job as a nonprofit fundraising consultant to stretch her legs and walk her black and tan Airedale Terrier.

As she walked, she tried to catch the eye of an attractive-looking man who was walking toward her on the sidewalk. He was wearing a gray fleece jacket and seemed completely absorbed by something on his phone.

The terrier pulled on his red leash to sniff around the base of a small maple tree. She looked away in respect for the terrier's privacy and read a flier for a missing cat that was stapled to the tree. With disappointment on her face, she thought, *Why would they use metal staples in a tree?*

The terrier, Fred, hunched up in the spot he felt was suitable in the small patch of grass carved out of the concrete sidewalk next to the curb. After a few moments, Fred was ready to move on. The young woman bent over with a green compostable bag covering her hand and scooped up Fred's midday constitutional that had been freshly deposited near the base of the tree.

She only briefly felt the touch of the Sig Sauer's suppressor that was now connected with the base of her skull while she was still bent over. The man in the gray fleece pulled the trigger twice out of a well-practiced habit.

She never knew what happened as she collapsed motionless to the ground with the red leash in one hand and the now full green bag in the other. The kill happened within the span of three heartbeats of the killer, the murderous act was mostly concealed by the parked cars at the curb.

The man in the gray jacket bent over to retrieve Fred's leash with a tug from the woman's hand, continuing to hold his Sig close to his thigh, as if nothing had happened. The killer led the dog along with him toward the next corner at Mulberry Street.

Chapter 37

Kostas and Marten arrived at the corner of Grace and Mulberry. They stopped for passing traffic, taking the opportunity to look both ways, seemingly at the vehicles passing.

As he did, he noticed a man in a gray jacket walking a dog across the street. Then, as he looked left, he slightly overextended his head to glimpse the distance of the two pursuers as he waited for traffic to clear.

In a whisper, Marten asked, "How far?"

"Within twenty yards. You will have to dodge the traffic with me."

As Kostas and Marten stepped off the curb to cross, a delivery van passed between them and the two men. Now momentarily out of sight of the pursuers, Kostas passed the Glock from his shoulder rig to Marten in one fluid motion. As he pulled the weapon, he turned it around, so the butt of the gun was presented to Marten's palm. He then carefully, but rapidly, pulled the smaller Glock 30 from his inside waistband holster, and they crossed the rest of the way to the corner at a quickened pace.

As they arrived at the next curb line, Kostas said to Marten, "In three. Mark…three… two… one."

Kostas broke left in a sprint over to the southeastern corner of the intersection, while Marten continued straight and took cover behind the front of a gray four-door Toyota Camry parked at the southwestern corner. The two pursuers became baffled halfway across the street, with traffic coming to a halt; neither of the two pursuers knew what to do or which way to go.

Kostas turned in mid-stride, acquiring his targets with his weapon and pulling his DoD credentials with his left hand. At the same time, Marten already had the Glock aimed across the top of the Camery in the direction of the two men.

Kostas yelled, "Federal Agent! Get down on the ground! Spread your arms and legs on the ground now!"

As traffic stopped, the two novice would be attackers complied, seeing no way out of double coverage with the two weapons aimed at them. Kostas moved forward to secure both assailants. Marten came out from the cover of the Camry as he noticed a small black and tan dog dragging a red leash, a surreal display that seemed so out of place with what was going on in the intersection. The dog passed between Marten and Kostas.

The sound of four swishes was audible to Kostas's ears; he recognized that sound. All four rounds from the suppressed weapon were now buried deep into the upper backs of the two men, face down in the middle of the crosswalk. Their arms still spread as pools of blood emerged from under both on the pavement.

Marten fired, then three more swishes were heard from the suppressed Sig Sauer P229. The first of the three dropped Marten to his knees, the second and third missed their mark as Kostas was already lunging for cover behind the rear driver's side of the same Camry that Marten had used initially for cover.

Kostas erupted from his cover but only saw a blur come across the Camery's trunk, then he felt a massive force hit him across his torso, knocking his weapon from his grasp.

As people ran from their abandoned cars, the terrier barked at the last two people alive in the intersection, now engaged in a life-and-death match. Both men rolled as they hit the ground, separating the two, then regained their feet just inches away from each other. The new assailant lunged at Kosta's midsection.

Kostas felt the pain in his lower back's old injury radiate like a fire from his hips down his legs. Not giving in to the pain, he instinctively sprawled his legs out, shifting the majority of his weight onto the foe's head and shoulders instead of allowing the man to gain an advantage by getting Kostas back on the ground.

He jammed his left arm under the attacker's right armpit and buried it up to the nook between his upper and lower arms. A move his high school wrestling coach called a whizzer.

Once Kostas felt the assailant struggle with the weight and force of Kostas's body, Kostas jammed the bony part of his right wrist under his opponent's nose with tremendous force, immediately causing it to burst in a spray of blood.

He then pushed with his left arm across his body while at the same time pulling with his right in the opposite direction. The attacker's face was now looking toward the sky instead of at the pavement, where it was only a second ago.

Kostas thrust his right foot forward. The synchronized move resulted in flipping the attacker on his back and to the ground, bringing Kostas's full force and weight squarely on the chest of the killer.

Kostas could see the attacker's suppressed Sig in reach next to an overflowing green metal trash can on the street corner; his Glock was nowhere to be found.

At a glance, he could see that the weapon was stovepiped; it had jammed. The last round fired had not fully ejected the brass and reloaded a new round into the chamber. That was why the attacker had abandoned it and resorted to hand-to-hand.

As the assassin tried to regain his breath after being pancaked to the ground with all of the one hundred and eighty-plus pounds of Kostas landing on him, Kostas released his grip with his right hand momentarily, then quickly pulled his three-inch bladed Spiderco knife that was clipped in his right pant pocket.

Using the thumb hole on the blade's top edge, he extended it in a fluid motion, locking the blade open. Then, he placed his thumb on the ridges that were machined into the blade's spine for grip and leverage.

With a strong purposeful thrust, Kostas buried the blade into the man's neck at an angle toward the brainstem, then twisted, heard a distinct pop, then pulled it across toward the man's Adam's apple.

The flow of blood was enormous. He had not hit the carotid artery, as he had hoped, only pushed it over with the pocketknife. However, he did enough tissue damage to the area that the flow of blood was rapid, but not a spray that would have resulted from the carotid being severed.

He gave the knife one more thrust upward in the wound; the man began to shake as if in a seizure.

Kostas pulled the knife out and slowly released the man. His back agonizing in fiery pain, he slowly came to one knee, then forced his way to his feet and scanned for any more threats. There were none.

He could hear sirens closing in. As his gaze drifted from the now dead man, he looked up to see a tall, slender blond woman in her mid to late twenties staring with her mouth agape in shock, holding a cell phone to her ear with one hand and a red dog leash in the other.

Kostas, in a bizarre thought given the circumstances around him, recognized the dog as some sort of tarrier. He then turned to Marten who lay there on the sidewalk, bent into a fetal position on his right side and paler than his naturally pale skin.

Kostas rushed to him to apply pressure to the wound. Marten opened his eyes and looked at Kostas, "I told you I didn't like that look on your face," he said through gritted teeth, then a series of coughs that produced a spattering of blood on the pavement.

"God damn you Marten you're going to be fine, hold in there. Think of Shane," he said as he removed his shirt to apply additional pressure on the wound.

Three Richmond police cruisers almost simultaneously arrived from three different directions: two from the east and west on Grace Street, one from the north on Mulberry, and moments later, an ambulance.

The young blond woman was now talking to one of the responding officers while holding the dog leash. Another walked west on Grace near a group of onlookers surrounding a now deceased former black and tan terrier owner.

More sirens could be heard approaching the intersection. As the medics took over the care of Marten, Kostas's voice commanded his phone to dial Wade, his fingers were useless on the phone's screen, being covered in Marten's and the assassin's blood. Before Wade could say hello or anything else, Kostas started recapping the last five minutes, which seemed like hours.

"After I give the locals a statement can you take care of the rest? They are approaching me now." Kostas asked Wade.

"I'll handle it as best as I can."

Kostas ended the call.

One of the officers had his phone out, presumably to record the conversation.

Body cam problem? Kostas thought to himself.

Kostas watched the ambulance with Marten pull away, not knowing his friend's future, then turned to the two approaching officers. Kostas identified himself after one of the officers validated the name on the credentials in the middle of the street.

One of the officers said, "We are going to have to keep your weapon for a time as evidence."

"I know the drill," Kostas replied.

Then he added, "There are two Glocks, one a forty-one and one a thirty. Both are mine. The Sig with the can on it belonged to the guy with his throat cut."

He continued to recap the events, starting with the sighting of the pickup truck with Michigan plates, referring to the commonly used term for a suppressor.

The younger of the two officers looked ill but continued to write down what Kostas said.

"The man in the ambulance, friend or foe?" the second officer asked.

"Friend."

"Is he also a Federal Agent?" the first officer asked.

"No, a friend that happened to be with me."

The younger officer wrote that down.

Kostas started to recap the events that led to three dead, and one critically injured, but the older officer seemed to want to show Kostas something on his phone. The officer swiped up on the screen, then turned it around so Kostas could see a picture.

Kostas felt the blood drain from his face. "I need to get home, now!" he said as he started limping toward Monument Avenue shirtless and covered in more than one man's blood.

The officer with the cell phone said, "I'm sure you do, and I am sure it's urgent. We will take you, you're in no shape to walk, and we still have a few more questions. Besides, your weapons are in evidence. I don't think you want to go anywhere without at least a officer and a weapon."

Kostas looked down at his shirtless torso, noticing the aftermath of the altercation for the first time. His jacket and shirt gone.

He then absently nodded. His lower back was in excruciating pain that radiated down his left leg, adding to that, the downhill slide of an adrenaline crash. He suddenly felt exposed and vulnerable and allowed himself to be escorted to a waiting K9 unit SUV.

As he sat in the front seat, he called Marika's cell, no answer, "Shit!"

He dialed Wade back, "I'm on my way to the house with a police escort." Then he told Wade what was on the officer's phone.

"I need Marika out of reach, and I need you to guarantee it with her leadership."

"What, a safe house?"

"No, I'll take care of the arrangements. I'll need your power to implement them, though. No one here can be trusted."

Wade agreed with a grunt.

"I'll see to the arrangements; just make sure she is cleared for absence due to national security."

He paused and winced in pain, then added, "I'll call you back, I am only a few blocks away."

"Done," came Wade's reply.

When the first two security gates of the driveway opened, Kostas attempted to jump from the officer's SUV as it rolled to a stop, but he could only manage a painful trot into the mudroom as the other two police cruisers sped up the driveway with their lights and sirens.

"MARIKA! MARIKA!" he called out.

She turned the corner from the basement stairs, her puzzled look turning into shock and worry as she absorbed his appearance.

"You need to leave the country," is all he said.

Chapter 38

"Όχι!" Marika replied. "No! I'm not leaving unless you're going with me! You're in more danger than I am!"

The two cruisers and the K-9 unit just pulled out of the driveway after clearing the house and getting Kostas's statement as Jess arrived with one of the MGSI security teams.

Before the police officers left Kostas's home, they said they received instructions to contact General Morris's office for additional information.

"I am bringing danger to you. This militia group will stop at nothing to get to me." He said.

"I don't care! If you're not going, I'm staying with you!"

Kostas took a deep breath that visibly caused more pain than it was worth.

He winced and said, "You can't."

He sat still, shirtless and covered in dried blood, "Let me show you what the Richmond police found."

He unlocked his cell phone and opened an email from Wade showing several surveillance photos of Kostas and Marika, not together, in separate places at separate times.

"These indicate that you're targeted, the photos don't just happen to have you in them because you were with me. They are of you."

Her eyes welled up with tears, "God damn it Kostas." she said in a tiny voice. "Look at you! You're too broken up to be left alone! You have to come with me!"

"You have to leave without me, I can't travel like this. I'll join you as soon as I can. Jess will have the security team watch over me. I promise I won't leave this fortress until my back is better."

He paused and said, "I know, it's not ideal. Just give me a few days to recover without worrying about your safety. I will follow then."

He winced again, "I love you, Marika."

She sniffled, "I love you too, this isn't fair. I can't lose you."

Ignoring the last part of her statement, he said, "Mikha'el Nikolaidis will be picking you up at the Port of Dublin, which will be your point of entry into Europe."

Referring to a close cousin of Kostas's, with whom he spent many summers during his childhood in Greece. Mikha'el graduated more than thirty years ago from the Merchant Marine Academy of Aspropyrgos, outside of Athens. He has been traveling the world as a licensed ship captain, mostly on cargo ships, ever since. They were still remarkably close to this day.

He continued, "After that, you won't need to process through any more passport control points on your way to Thessaloniki. Jess and her handpicked team will accompany you to Ireland and ensure you are handed off successfully to Frank Cromwell with MI6. Frank will ensure you get on Mikha'el's ship and provide security from Dublin to their final destination in Singapore."

"Wait, you said Thessaloniki, not Singapore?" Marika asked, confused.

"That's right. You will be getting off in Thessaloniki with the rest of the MI6 security team. The ship will continue without you to Singapore, but no one will know that." he said in a reassuring voice.

Moving slightly to adjust his back, he groaned, "Frank owes me a few favors, and this whole investigation has the British Government's concern up, too, not just ours here in the US."

Kostas replied, omitting the fact that the disembarkation from the cargo ship to the Greek mainland would take place in the middle of the night via helicopter, courtesy of a nearby UK SAS Team conducting hunt and kill operations on pirates in the Mediterranean.

She reached for a tissue and blew her nose. In a feeble attempt at humor, she asked, "No lake?"

Kostas smiled, hugged her through the pain, and whispered, "Next time."

Chapter 39

Kostas watched from his house's window as the four identical Ford SUVs with darkened windows pulled through the driveway's first two security gates and back to the rear of his home.

He went to the mudroom in the rear of the house, grabbed Marika's duffle bag, and winced in pain as he picked it up. Marika admonished him with a look and snatched it from his hand. "You know better than that! You're hurt! You keep doing stuff like that, I'll stay right here!"

Kostas forced a smile and said, "I love you and I will follow as soon as I can." He hugged her. "Remember the plan, right?"

"I remember, but I don't like it. You should be coming with me, but I remember," she said sullenly.

Then, after a long sigh, she recited, "I am to get in the vehicle with Jess, the SUVs will take turns changing positions on Monument Avenue until they reach Willow Lawn, where they will split into two groups, one north to Broad Street, the other south to Patterson Avenue. Then, each of the two teams will eventually find its way to Richmond International Airport. One decoy with Hendricks and a support unit, the other me, Jess, and the security team."

"Correct. They will drive directly onto the aircraft ramp at the old Sandston Guard unit, where a private flight will be waiting in the main hangar. Following suit, all the SUVs will drive directly into the hangar with you. Once the last SUV is in, the hangar doors will be closed and not open until you and the team are onboard, and the aircraft is ready for taxi. The next stop is Dublin."

She sighed again, "You better be close behind me, Kostas."

"I will as soon as I am able. You have the Glock?"

"In the holster, with two extra mags."

She got on her tippy toes to kiss him as she patted the holster on her right hip below her jacket. "I love you."

Jess interrupted, "It's time."

"I love you too." And they were gone.

Chapter 40

Jess had agreed to Kostas's demand for the no-comms policy while in transport, so there would be no triangulation of transmissions to determine which SUV was the decoy team and which one was not.

Everyone was expected to just stick to the plan.

As soon as they were out of the last gate and it closed, Kostas sprinted the best he could up the stairs, changing from his sweats and T-shirt to his traveling clothes. He grabbed his phone and the prescriptions for his back pain on the kitchen counter. Then he exited the mudroom door to the garage, where Jess had left a black duffle bag with a red handle.

Kostas knew that there would be hell to pay once Marika realized that he had been playing up his injury. But he needed to get her out of harm's way, especially after what happened to Marten.

He needed to focus on what he knew how to do best: "I search, and I find."

He unzipped the canvas duffle and tossed the two bottles of meds for his back in it—one a strong anti-inflammatory and the other a nerve block. Then he walked into the garage and threw the duffle into the truck's passenger seat. His next stop was Marquette Sawyer Regional Airport in the Upper Peninsula of Michigan.

As Kostas approached the front gate on Falcon Drive, the gate guard, recognizing the truck and Kostas, smiled and saluted him.

Jess was in charge of the timelines and coordinated MGSI's resources with Hendricks. She meticulously planned the routes so that Kostas could get to the airport after Marika and her.

He parked outside the Ops building again and was driven to one of the two smaller alert hangars on the left of the aircraft ramp.

Once on board the small white aircraft with no tail markings other than an American flag, he texted Wade, "Boarded."

As the crew prepped Kostas's aircraft in the alert hanger only a few hundred yards away from Marika and Jess's aircraft, the co-pilot walked back to Kostas and said, "General Morris is on the line. You can take it in the rear SCIF."

Then motioned to the rear of the aircraft. "There is a seat that you can buckle in there for takeoff. Oh, and your comms are secure, Sir, and won't be interrupted as we taxi and take off. "Please secure your duffle with you in the SCIF," he added.

Kostas nodded and said, "Thank you. What's the status of the cargo's transport?"

"They are ready to taxi, Sir. The cargo is now being loaded and secured. Their hangar door is being opened now. We will wait for them to get airborne, then we will start our own taxi," came back the reply.

"Thank you, I'll be in the back until we arrive at the destination," Kostas said.

"Copy that. Our flight plan calls for us to refuel and wait for you, General's orders." The co-pilot replied and then returned to the cockpit, indicating it was a statement not up for negotiation.

Chapter 41

As Kostas sat in the soon-to-be-airborne SCIF, he buckled the seatbelt, placed the headset on his head, and adjusted the boom-style mic in front of his mouth. Then, he logged in to the computer, and Wade's image was shown on the screen.

"Well, it's not the Air Guard that you requested last time," said Wade.

"It's not an Army Guard Black Hawk either," Kostas replied.

"No, it is not. Neither is the cargo's aircraft," was all Wade said.

Confirming Kostas's speculation of so-called off the books US Government assets with a global reach that even the FBI did not have knowledge of, let alone tracking of.

Then Wade added, "The cargo just left the hangar and is the only craft cleared to move on the airfield."

Kostas gave a single nod to the screen.

"You have everything you need?" asked Wade.

Kostas nodded into the camera again.

"Good. We have two other teams deployed actively and ready to ride when needed from the north."

"The north? Canucks?"

"No, the 160th Night Stalkers, to be exact," refers to the elite aviation regiment renowned for its proficiency in night operations and helicopter missions. They routinely operate with the cover of night to insert, support, and extract special operation forces in high-risk areas.

Wade added, "Of course, I added something special in there for you." Wade grinned.

"And that is?"

Still grinning with pride, Wade said, "The 1st SFOD-D."

"Delta Team? Deployed on US soil? You're kidding me. Don't get me wrong, seeing some of the guys again will be good, but how did you pull that off?" Kostas asked, intrigued.

Again, displaying enormous pride in how he pulled this off, Wade replied, "Typically, the Posse Comitatus Act of 1878 would prohibit them from operating on US soil. However, there are now exceptions to that, thanks to events like 9/11."

His grin widened, "Obviously, training and advisory roles are one exception, but also national emergencies and counterterrorism operations. In her infinite wisdom, President Adams again classified our investigation as a counterterrorism operation with the Executive Order she issued."

"Careful that smile may be permanent if you don't tone it down," Kostas said in jest.

"Those are some of the only assets that I can command besides the one you and the cargo are sitting in without too much outside knowledge or approvals."

Kostas nodded in understanding.

"There is also a US Navy Littoral Combat Ship currently in Lake Superior conducting joint training exercises with the Coast Guard and Customs and Border Patrol. You and the teams have an assigned bay for briefings and gear prepping."

"You're making this easy for me, Wade."

"Am I? There is too much riding on all of this. This mission cannot fail."

Both men paused.

Then, after a brief silence, Kostas asked, "Any info on the attack on Marten and me?"

"Yes, the first two are a couple of nobodies who drove their own vehicles from Michigan. They had two handguns with them holstered in the small of their backs, and a twelve-gauge shotgun and zip tie restraints in the truck. I feel confident that Marten was not a target."

Kostas interrupted solemnly, "I know, they were after me."

"Right, so forget the pity party before it begins. You have a job to do, Alpha." Wade barked, proving that Kostas was wrong about the smile being permanent.

Kostas just stared at the screen.

Wade continued, "Both are low-level goons in the militia. The truck has been in Virginia for a while, picked up on traffic cams in the Fredericksburg and Spotsylvania areas over the last three months."

"The North Anna Nuclear Plant surveillance team?"

"Don't know, could be, but I agree with you and Jess's assessment of the intel and counter-intel on North Anna. One other thing about Tweetle Dee and Tweetle Dub in the pickup truck, the forensics team at my request combed over the truck, and in the floorboard's mats they found traces of a subunit protein, which tested positive for the Ricin B Chain."

Ricin B is the second component of the two required to weaponize the chemical Agent Ricin. The B Chain binds to certain carbohydrates in the body and on the surface of its cells. Then, it facilitates the entry of the second component, or A Chain, into the cells by binding to the cell's surface receptors and promoting endocytosis, or the process that allows cells to intake nutrients and other molecules.

"Shit. Do you think it's similar to the Tajikistan border operation in Afghanistan?" Kostas asked with a grimace.

"There is only one way to find out. And that, my friend, is why your recon mission to the UP of Michigan is now a larger operation."

"Shit."

"Given the new circumstances, I took the liberty to request Tom Krause to lead the Deltas. With a potential Ricin threat, I figured you could use him there."

"Thanks, what about the third guy, the shooter? The guy who shot Marten?" Kostas asked.

"Konrad or Kurt Vista. A former FBI Agent who left the Bureau shortly after the current administration took office. He seemed to have a different opinion on the new administration's direction and policies than the former administration. He has been performing freelance assassinations for militant groups, both foreign and domestic, as well as other less-than-savory organizations since separating from the Bureau. You got lucky; his official file reads like an all-star or Hall of Fame quarterback's resume of accomplishments. The Sig still had eight rounds in the magazine. Forensics' tests show the stove-piping of the last round fired was likely due to the back pressure of the suppressor and a subsonic round that had a light load of gunpowder that subsequently caused him to abandon the weapon."

Nodding again, Kostas said, "Wouldn't cycle the next round because it didn't have enough energy to eject the last round's brass fully."

"Bingo!" Wade exclaimed, then continued, "Knowing you had your weapon already pulled and hadn't even fired a single round yet, he likely made a split-second decision to attack you hand-to-hand and not take the time to cycle the slide on the weapon to dislodge the stuck brass and rack a new round."

Continuing to nod while looking thoughtfully at the screen, Kostas said, "Yeah, gutsy move, it was a gamble. Either take the time with both hands to clear the stuck brass, then cycle the slide to load another round, as I am sure he was trained to do, or fight hand-to-hand. Experience must have weighed in on the decision. We had to be only ten or fifteen yards away from each other at that point; if that. By the time he tilted the weapon and got his thumb and forefinger on the slide, I was likely to already break my cover and fire."

Now shaking his head he added, "Tough call, I'm glad I didn't have to make that call."

"Yeah, me too," said Wade, then continued, "It looks like he was either sent as a backup in case tweetle dee and dumb failed, or just to get rid of them as two loose ends or complications.

After reading the report Jess sent over on the counter-intel and what she called a rabid dog, I tend to think Vista was there to stop and discourage any future ideas of taking matters on the ground into the low-level leader's own hands without higher authorization. The question is, who brought Vista in?"

Kostas nodded thoughtfully in front of the screen and said, "I can think of a person or two."

"Right, and that brings me to Operation Limey Sparrow, by the way, I love the name," Wade said.

"Yeah, with everything going on near the house and with Marten, Jess hadn't had a chance to brief me."

Wade started, "Well, Hogan stayed in the restaurant to make a call for almost thirty minutes after you left. Jess captured your conversation with Hogan and the phone call after you left with the 'long-eared' listening device. Then she began to tail Hogan at that point."

Wade paused and thought for a moment then said, "Now I didn't have video to go along with the audio, but from what I could hear; damn she did try her best to get something out of you."

Wade laughed then continued, "After you left, Hogan was talking to an individual who was using a burner phone without a doubt. The individual was male and older. The voice was somewhat distorted using a concealment app on the phone. Obviously wanting to avoid voice recognition, Hogan's voice is clear as day, telling him that her attempt to right the ship didn't go as planned. She assured the other voice that she would continue to pursue that course until it was a dead end. We feel confident it was likely Lawrence Johnson."

Kostas's dark and slightly graying eyebrows rose over his eyes, "I guess I can take the dead end part to heart."

"I would," Wade replied, then continued, "Jess followed Hogan to DC, an office building for the concrete company owned by Lawrence Johnson. Jess used the opportunity to install a GPS tracking device on Hogan's vehicle.

Then she followed Hogan to her home just over the West Virginia border in Charles Town. A modest three-bedroom town home, emblematic of her salary and tenure at the Bureau, nothing out of the ordinary. We have satellite assets watching it, no human ground units. I didn't want to risk them being found out. Frank and MI6 deployed a Stingray operation on Hogan's phone at Jess's informal request." Referring to an application that mimics cell towers and can be used to track the location of a mobile phone.

Kostas smiled and once again thought of giving Jess a bonus, then said, "Interesting twist. The Bureau is going to be pissed that one of their cars, let alone an Agent's phone was tapped."

"A corrupt Agent— fuck'em. This is my investigation." Wade said, then added, "Now for the rest of the Limey part of the investigation. I'll keep it to the important parts; the Brits found a link to Lawrence Johnson and Hogan in their investigation of the FBI assets on the task force.

"How bad is it?" asked Kostas.

"Hogan was on a team charged with investigating domestic militia groups for the Bureau after 911. It was a logical follow-up to the terrorist cell investigations here in the United States. MI6 tied the timelines for Hogan to the Johnson brothers' activities. Same dates, same general locations. During her official leave of absence from the FBI, they also had hits on Hogan's personal credit cards and debit cards for restaurants and hotels in the southeastern region of Michigan and around Lawrence Johnson's DC office."

"Leave of absence?"

"Yeah, bereavement."

Kostas, looking puzzled, said, "Wade, you lost me."

Frank theorized that somehow, she obtained firsthand knowledge of the brothers through her investigation and became radicalized against the US Government after the death of her sister."

"Her sister?" What does that have to do with any of this?

"I'm so glad you asked. I have to hand it to Frank and his people over at MI6; they really delivered on this one." Wade added, then paused.

Looking impatient, Kostas asked, "Well?"

"Her sister Karen committed suicide after the death of her husband." Then Wade paused again.

"Ok, not uncommon. Sad, but not uncommon when one spouse dies." Kostas replied.

"True, but when your Air Force husband dies in his thirties from colon cancer and you blame the United States Government for it, then off yourself; well, that can set up a scenario that could derail a surviving sister from the reasonable rails of life."

"Wait." Realization dawning on Kostas. "Karen Chilcott was Hogan's sister? Bobby Chilcott's wife?"

"Yes, evidently Hogan spent a lot of time with Bobby being supportive while he was sick. Taking him to appointments and running errands for him while Karen was either at work or mentally exhausted with everything that Bobby was going through. Frank's investigation found doctor office appointment sign-ins by Hogan and a power of attorney naming Hogan to Bobby's medical needs in addition to his wife. MI6 also found several letters that Karen Chilcott wrote to the Air Force, her congressman, and even the SecDef blaming the Government for Bobby's cancer and death."

Now Kostas could see the clues that had been there all along. They began to click into a mental puzzle behind his eyes.

Wade continued, "Frank also theorized that in Bobby's condition and knowing Hogan was an Agent with a high-level security clearance, he may have talked about Project Paratiro as he would to an old military buddy on his deathbed. Frank also produced evidence that Hogan and her sister were extremely close and basically raised each other in an abusive home environment. Hogan was the older sister by just over a year and was very protective of the younger Karen."

"So Hogan, while grieving the death of Bobby and her sister, found a way to avenge their deaths."

"That's the way I'm seeing it. After Karen's death, Hogan took an extended leave of absence due to bereavement. Her whereabouts during that leave of absence are officially unknown. That being said, I would put odds on Frank's theory that she grieved to a pair of sympathetic ears with the Johnson brothers. At that point, *Alea iacta est*."

Nodding, Kostas translated in understanding, "The die was cast."

Then added, "That's how she knew about DTRA's Washington Technical Support Group and what Verum-I Perlustro Verum-I Reperrlo means. I search the truth; I find the truth."

Wade tacked on, "Correct, and knowing the translation of the word Paratiro, to observe, and its tie to DTRA. Then add to that the fact that she was late in identifying Rizzarreo, when we both know she could have identified him hours earlier by the dog tag laced up in his boot, as you pointed out in the initial briefing."

Kostas leaned in closer to the monitor, "She delayed the identification of the body to allow the rest of the teams their escape. Then reported back to her terrorist bastard friends that I was brought in on the investigation and that I was the person who shot Rizzarreo on the I-95 scene."

Kostas paused, and then something occurred to him: "The North Anna MISP scenario was one of Bobby's contributions to Program Paratiro. Bobby might have told her all the scenarios that we worked on back then."

Wade agreed with a nod and then added, "Bobby's scenario involved the storming of the North Anna Nuclear Facility with a small contingency of well-trained terrorists to cause the reactor to meltdown, which, depending on the weather and wind direction, could have devastated the Virginia region as well as everything downwind."

With disdain, Kostas spat out, "Similar, if not worse than, the devastation of Chernobyl 1986. His scenario hinged greatly on a terrorist team penetrating through all the security measures and gaining control of the operations of the facility before a counter strike could be deployed by us, which would heavily depend on, first, the complete knowledge of the layout of the facility, including which rooms were where and what hallways led to what. Not exactly public information."

Kostas added, "The second critical component of the scenario was how to override the safety protocols that were in place, then trigger an unrecoverable meltdown of the reactor's core. It would take someone with a high level of technical knowledge in the operations of a nuclear power plant, not just a theorist or a bad guy with ill intent."

"Exactly." Wade agreed. "Given the high level of technical knowledge that would be needed to pull it off, the whole scenario was deemed unlikely to take place and relegated to the low-risk of occurrence category in the program. Again, the problem statement asked how a foreign terrorist group could attack the Capital region, not a group of domestic terrorists or insurrectionists trying to overthrow the US Government. However, our current domestic enemy could in fact recruit former or current workers in the facility or within the Department of Energy itself."

"Hell, the DOE is a big organization; people are always retiring or leaving for other jobs, making them available for recruiting," Kostas replied.

It was Wade's turn to nod, then he said, "We narrowly avoided a massive radiation incident that would have killed tens of thousands, if not more, thanks to your idea to move up DTRA's joint training exercises at North Anna and Oak Ridge, then behind the scenes substitute the training exercises for the real-world mission."

"Thank the DTRA Washington Technical Support Group, not me. They were the ones who mobilized at a moment's notice and successfully defended the sites." Kostas said, then felt the aircraft engines surge and the plane start to move.

He hesitated momentarily and asked, "Where is Hogan now?"

Wade recognized the change in Kostas's face on the screen. "Start your preflight breathing ritual, don't talk, just listen to me."

Kostas nodded in agreement.

"Marika and Jess are now airborne," Wade interjected.

Kostas nodded and asked again, "Where is Hogan now?"

"She is still under surveillance. Currently, she is in the Washington Field Office and isn't going anywhere without us knowing about it."

In an icy tone, Kostas said, "Good. I have one more mission after this current one— take down Hogan. I want to be the one who takes her down, Wade."

Wade nodded.

Kostas felt the aircraft turn during taxi and begin to gain ground speed rapidly.

Taking a deep breath and then exhaling, Kostas asked, "Any updates on W?"

"He is doing his normal thing on the campaign trail. Nothing new to update you on. To be honest, I think he is clean of all of this."

Skeptical Kostas replied, "Maybe. It could be a radical right faction that is just in favor of his administration."

"That's what I am thinking," Wade added.

"All right, we just went weight off wheels. I'll let you know when we land." Kostas said with a shade of color that was paler than his complexion.

Wade nodded and then severed the communications.

Chapter 42

He rushed out of his Duke Street office building, untying his colorfully patterned tie, which his wife and kids had given him for his birthday last year. He carefully rolled it up and placed it in his satchel-style laptop bag.

If he hurried, he could make happy hour at Theismann's across from the King Street Metro Station before the last train left to connect with the Virginia Rail Express, or VRE. He ordered a Tito's and tonic, double tall. He texted his wife that he was at the metro and would be home soon. He took his first sip of the drink, hoping to put behind him a stressful and seemingly unproductive day. Jack Flanagan paid his tab in cash, leaving the rest of the twenty-dollar bill as a tip on the sixteen-dollar drink.

As the train cars slowed to a stop at the Van Dorn Metro Station, he texted his wife once again. "Metro on time," the reply came back with a red heart emoji.

As Jack sat and thumbed through the rest of the emails that he hadn't had the chance to read earlier in the day, he thought about the more than six years he had spent commuting to his nonprofit employer.

"This is getting old." He muttered to himself, then let out a long breath.

Jack knew he spent too much time commuting and not enough time with his wife and three small children.

He overheard someone in the train car say, "So glad the metro and the VRE are back running." He smiled and went back to his emails.

Three men in extremely expensive suits, likely costing a week's salary for most people, were standing on the railway platform at the Franconia-Springfield Station, waiting for the Fredericksburg Line of the VRE. Their black designer laptop backpacks rested with a single sling uniformly positioned across each of their left shoulders. Jack thought the scene resembled an ad for some new menswear launching for the fall collection and targeted at the DC Beltway elite.

Chapter 43

Kostas's plane landed, and the aircraft rolled to a stop at the small regional airport as he removed his seatbelt and stopped his four count breathing.

The airfield first opened in 1955 as K.I. Sawyer Air Force Base was historically the home of several Cold War-era units for the Air Force's B-52 Stratofortress bombers and KC-135 Stratotanker aircraft. These aircraft served as a crucial nuclear deterrence strategy against the then Soviet Union. Now it was a small municipal airport that housed a maintenance hub for a subsidiary of American Airlines and other local businesses.

As he walked to the front of the aircraft with his duffle, the co-pilot opened the boarding door and lowered the stairs. "Sir, we will refuel and be ready for takeoff when you are. I took the liberty of letting General Morris know we landed."

"Thank you," Kostas said with a handshake.

"God speed, Sir." Then the co-pilot headed back to the cockpit.

Chapter 44

"Project Tube in place?" asked the voice on the other end of the phone.

"Yes, everything is in order and on time," replied the other man's voice.

"Any loose ends?" the first voice asked.

"None at this point. The team lead will handle it on site if there are."

Then added, "The local team already set up egresses."

The other voice said approvingly, "Excellent. Let's hope this goes a long way toward our goals. The American people need to see that there is only one man in the race who can turn this country around."

The second voice replied, "God bless OUR Nation."

"God bless OUR Nation." The caller agreed, then hung up.

Chapter 45

Kostas carried his duffle bag across the tarmac to a small, unoccupied maintenance shed. He dialed Jess's number.

"All well?" he asked.

"As planned, by me, I might I add," she said confidently.

"I'll give you this quarter's MVP award. Seriously, though, Jess, I knew you would be the only one to pull off the planning and logistics, as well as the execution. And the cargo? What's her status?"

"Incredibly pissed at you and the situation as expected. We have about two hours to wheels down." Jess reported.

"And the decoy?" He asked.

"Frank and his team are set. Either way, I believe it was worth the deception. I'll part ways with the cargo and the escort team and then rendezvous with you as conditions dictate."

"Copy," he replied.

"Hey Kostas, the cargo has been briefed for comms and would like to get on the line."

There was a brief pause and Kostas heard Marika's voice, "God damn you Kostas; you wait until I see you!"

He couldn't help but smile at her voice, even if it was in a tone of anger.

During the planning of the operation to get Marika to safety, Kostas asked Jess to brief Marika on the plan once they were airborne, but only part of it. He had exaggerated his back injury, knowing that was the only way to get Marika out of harm's way. He also knew she would be furious with him, but understood that she would never leave unless he portrayed himself as too injured to travel and would be safe under the security team's watch at home.

Kostas and Jess were the only two who knew the complete plan from A to Z. Not even Wade knew all the details. Once on the plane in Richmond, Marika was only referred to as the cargo. That cargo would land in Shannon, Ireland, where Frank's team would meet her, and Jess would hand her off. Not as scheduled, a hundred and thirty-seven miles away in Dublin.

Frank would then helicopter her to the USS Ramage, where a team of US SEALs would wait to escort her by another helicopter once the Ramage was close to Greece's coastline in the Ionian Sea, just south of the island of Corfu.

Once on the mainland of Greece, Kostas's friends in the Hellenic 32nd Marine Brigade from the port town of Volos would accept 'custody' of the cargo, and the SEALs would part ways and return to the Ramage.

During the cargo exchange, Marika's call sign was now known as Hera, the goddess often called the 'Queen of Olympus' in Greek mythology.

Kostas's new call sign became Zeus.

The commander of the 32nd Marine Brigade took his job and his missions seriously. Historically, the Hellenic Marine Brigade spent time training with elite US units like SEALs, Deltas, USAF Combat Controllers, and other allied special units in Europe.

These training missions that turned into real-world missions over time created bonds that transcended not just years but politics and, at times, a need for 'official written orders.'

Kosta's previous military career put him in situations where these bonds were formed, and now, he uses them.

"Will I be punished?" Kostas quipped back to Marika over the phone with a smile.

"Yes, but not how you want to be!" she spat into the phone, "Can I at least know where I will end up waiting for you?"

"Yes, Jess will fill you in completely once you land. But you'll recognize it, think of that time we were drinking coffee on Route 82 together."

Kostas was referring to a small coffee shop and sports bar that Kostas's cousin owned and operated in Litochoro, Greece, Route 82. Not the well known San Francisco highway that runs to San Jose, California.

She paused, "Are you kidding me?"

"Nope."

With a crack in her voice, she replied, "Come back to me, I mean it! Safe! With all your parts!"

"I will, see you as soon as I can." Then he clicked off.

Chapter 46

A mother and her eight-year-old daughter rushed through the turnstiles at the Franconia-Springfield Metro. Mary Rosenburg had a late afternoon meeting that ran past its scheduled one hour with a client interested in partnering on a new requirement for IT modernization at the IRS. She almost missed the cutoff time to pick up her daughter from after-school childcare.

Doing her best as a single mom and trying to climb the corporate ladder tugged at her every emotion simultaneously, all in different directions.

As she sat down in the metro car's seat and unslung her laptop bag, she placed it on her lap. Then, she let out an exasperated sigh. She noticed her daughter mimicking this entire act. She forced a smile but thought to herself, *What kind of example am I setting?*

Mary made room in the crowded car by shifting her knees and bag for a tall, barrel-chested man dressed in worn jeans and a flannel shirt. She noticed old, worn military boots at the end of his bulky frame.

She recognized the type of boots he wore; they were almost identical to her deadbeat ex-husband's boots, who had served in the US Army for a little less than four years.

The man in the boots stood holding the metal bar with his left hand, which was attached to her seat near the automated doors of the train car. With his other hand, he held a black canvas duffel bag that looked heavy and had odd angles pushed outward on its canvas walls.

Mary watched the man place the duffle on the floor of the car and pull out a set of what looked to be earbuds from his pant pocket. He placed them into his ears and carefully pulled out his cell phone from the flannel's left breast pocket, holding the metal bar tightly with the other hand.

Over the noise of the train car's movement on the tracks, Mary heard him say to someone on the phone, "On time," then he thumbed through screens on his phone.

Chapter 47

The UH-60 Black Hawk hadn't fully touched down when Kostas tossed his duffle and pack to the crew chief to secure them in the helicopter. He started to board when a gloved hand from inside the helicopter reached out to him. He took it at the forearm and was hoisted into the craft.

The man in black tactical gear, with a full beard and a big smile, looked at Kostas and said, "Alpha."

Kostas replied, "Tom, good to see you."

Thomas Krause, now a seasoned Delta with the Army's 1st Special Forces Operational Detachment or 1st SFOD-D. First met Kostas in the northeastern region of Afghanistan near the Tajikistan border. Tom, then in his early twenties, served on an Air Force Combat Control Team or CCT.

CCTs operated true to their motto, *'First There,'* as highly trained air traffic controllers capable of managing air strikes and air-to-ground support while operating on the ground in hostile environments, often deep behind enemy lines.

These highly trained air traffic controllers did not sit in air-conditioned towers overlooking airfields; they were truly first in with other Special Operations units and deadly in their own right.

Either by parachuting or rappelling from helicopters behind enemy lines, they had almost everything they needed strapped to their bodies.

All the communication gear and warfighting equipment came into the area of operation with them to efficiently set up air support, landing zones, and rescue operations behind enemy lines with deadly results.

Several years after their first encounter near the Tajikistan border and at the urging of current Deltas he had met, Krause applied to the Army's elite 1st SFOD-D and was accepted formally, transferring from the United States Air Force to the Army.

Through his smile and beard, Krause said, "Wade said you two needed a hand."

"That we do, Tom, and I hope it is more than just hoisting me into a helicopter. Can you give me a rundown on the team?"

"Before I do, you still remember how to reload an AK-47?" Tom said with his big grin.

"I may have forgotten the first lesson, but I never forgot the second one. Thanks for busting my balls as soon as I got on the chopper." Kostas replied.

As the Black Hawk ascended and followed the runway for takeoff, Kostas donned the helmet that included comms while quietly Box Breathing.

"You all right?" Krause said into the mic.

Kostas said, "Never better, Tom. The team?"

"Right, as requested by Wade, we have two teams, six in each. You round out the total to make it a lucky thirteen. Three operators you already know: Montgomery, Smith, and Moore. The rest came into Delta after you left active duty. All the newbies have been blooded and are top-notch. You have my word."

"And Wade's instructions to the team?"

"Sit with the Canucks on their mainland until you touch down at the old K.I. Airstrip. Rendezvous with you and follow your lead after we get to the Littoral."

Kostas gave a single nod. "Surveillance?"

"Satellite updated every hour; drones are being paused until you call for them. We have access to all of their comms and are monitoring them from the Littoral. It seems they are excited about something. There is a lot of chatter, but not any buildup or actions within the compound that would indicate knowledge of our operation. It seems like something else has their panties in a bunch. We had a scouting team evaluate the entrances and the perimeter last night. We have a full brief ready for you when we land."

Again, a single nod from Kostas. The trip over Lake Superior was incredibly beautiful and at the same time extremely terrifying for Kostas.

As he glimpsed the northern coastline approaching, he texted Wade, "I can smell maple syrup from where I am." A thumbs up emoji and a "Tell Tom hi." That was all he received in return.

Chapter 48

Matt Hudlebac tightened his grip on the metal bar. He had almost lost his balance and fallen into the lap of a young mother and her daughter as he called his husband to say he would be home on time.

He thumbed at his phone, looking for his news app, and then clicked live. The featured news piece was already in progress. It was a presidential candidate at a campaign rally saying, "This would never happen on my watch. Terrorists on US soil, never. They wouldn't dare on my watch."

Matt shook his head, frowned, and closed the news app. He then selected a playlist on Spotify and turned up the volume on his earbuds. It was Mozart's *Eine Kleine Nachtmusik* or A Little Night Music. Matt picked up his tool bag and closed his eyes, then let the motion of the rail car rock him to the enjoyment of the music.

Chapter 49

Kostas and the two Delta Force Teams assembled in an unoccupied mission bay below the Littoral's rear flight deck. Krause walked up to the makeshift briefing room's whiteboard.

"OK, team, we have six leadership targets, including one known as Red Johnson. All of you have your deck of playing cards for tonight's game, memorize their faces. Here are our objectives: one, remove command and control. Two, destroy all food, water, and armament stockpiles to convince the occupants in the compound that it's a bad idea to dig in. Last, three, identify, document, and destroy chemical weapon manufacturing capabilities for Ricin. We have intel that both Ricin chains A and B are located within the compound."

Referring to the two critical elements needed to weaponize the deadly substance, which, when introduced to the body, will result in circulatory collapse and organ failure within the victim. Death follows slowly and painfully in three to five days after exposure.

"I will be leading Wraith-One, who will execute the rendition operation, and Wraith-Two will be on demo, led by Montgomery.

Hear me and understand me when I say, General Morris personally told me not to let this turn into, and I am using his words; 'some god damn Waco fucking Texas incident!'"

Kostas thought to himself, *that's a damn good impression of Wade.*

Krause looked around the room. "Any questions at this point?"

Silence is all he heard in return. With a single nod, Krause continued, "Here are the assignments and the details. Objective one: Five of the six senior leaders reside with their families in a two-story, small apartment building. Evidently rank has its privileges even in scumbag militias."

A few small chuckles echoed in the hangar.

"As you can see here on the last hour's satellite imagery, the rest of the compound's occupants are housed in building seven here, another two-story structure,"

Krause used a green targeting laser he pulled from his MP5's accessory rail to highlight the area on a large monitor. "And also in its twin, building twelve here. Neither is a threat, given their distance away from our buildings of interest. We will be going in silence and at night."

A few of the team members gave each other high-fives and fist bumps.

Krause continued, "We will be incapacitating the targets and their families with a knockout gas. No lethality is authorized in Objective One unless absolutely necessary for mission success. Trust me, you will find yourself off this team and on a desk as a supply clerk if you violate this needlessly. These are Americans, regardless of their claim to sovereignty or any other bullshit they spout. Did I make myself clear?"

There was a chorus of head nods and grunts in agreement.

He continued, "Get the targets, leave the rest for the local authorities. Approximately two hours after the gas is deployed, the families will wake with a nasty hangover and their wrists bound. The sixth target, Red Johnson, lives above the armory on the second floor, north of the firing range. His living quarters are connected to his office overlooking the range. His snatch will also use knockout gas to facilitate; he has a history as a LEO and knows how to use every weapon at his disposal. All targets will be thoroughly searched for weapons and anything of use for Intel. All targets will be secured in a rendition style, hoods and zip ties to the wrists, elbows, ankles, and knees, then extracted on our mobile litters behind the electronic bikes that are prepositioned in the drop zone."

He paused to survey the audience and then continued, "According to the intel folks, Lawrence Johnson is not suspected of being in the compound. However, all of you have your deck of cards; if you see him, snag him. Double up the litters if you have to, bring an extra cargo strap for all I care." Several team members laughed.

He paused again for questions, hearing none, Krause pressed on, "Now, after Objective One's targets have been secured for transport and we are all clear from the site, all electronics within the compound will be disabled via an EMP, or electromagnetic pulse generating device developed recently by DARPA. To pull this off, we have *borrowed* a local power company utility truck that is prepositioned over three miles away, staffed with Army National Guard personnel who were brought in from DTRA's Headquarters to ensure there are no militia sympathizers among them. Once the compound is disconnected from the rest of the electrical grid, the device nicknamed 'The Big Blip' will send an electromagnetic pulse across the power lines leading into the compound so powerful it will fry any circuit board from within six feet of an electrical outlet or wire. This includes backup generators and cell phones. Don't be inside the fence when this happens; your comms will be rendered inoperable. It goes without saying that the power will be out for a long time around here. But more importantly for the bad guys, all communication devices, computers, and radios will be rendered useless. Even electric well pumps will be inoperable."

One of the Deltas snorted and said, "Much more practical and precise than having an EA-18 Growler or the old EF-111 fly over to do it."

Krause interrupted, "You finished yet Garnett?"

"Yes, Sergeant Major," Garnett replied respectfully.

"Good, may I continue now?" asked Krause.

"Yes, Sergeant Major."

"Thank you. Now, are there any questions at this point?" asked Krause.

"Sergeant Major, who is the old dude?" asked one of the youngest Deltas. He was in his thirties and had the stature and smile of a young, arrogant soldier with several successful missions behind him.

An 'oh no he didn't…' murmuring fell over the group.

Montgomery took one step toward the soldier and with a right cross clocked him across the jaw, staggering him a bit.

She then said in an unmistakable tone of authority and experience, "That is Alpha, and that is all you need to know. If he speaks to you, you listen. If he says go fuck yourself, you better start trying. You got that?"

The young man, still getting his bearings back from the punch, wiped a little blood from the corner of his mouth and nodded.

Montgomery asked again, "You got it?"

"I got it, I got it." He replied dumbly.

With a smile, Krause looked around, "To clarify Montgomery's answer for you, Holt, the old dude is Kostas Papadopoulos, call sign Alpha. Now, are there any other questions? No? OK, on to Objective Two."

Kostas couldn't help but allow a slight grin at the young man's tactical misstep.

"Montgomery and her Wraith-Two team will be eliminating centuries in their path, lethal force authorized as required. Then, the incendiary charges for building two, which serves as a dining facility and food storage, will be set. Again, incendiary charges will be used to maximize the devastation and confusion of the enemy and minimize casualties. Same for building nine, the armory. Just blowing it up will not ensure that the number of weapons and ammo stored there will be rendered useless. We need to ensure that local law enforcement and other agencies are not outgunned after we egress. We know from human intel gathering that Red is extremely specific on the control and access to the weapons. He likes to sleep over the top of the armory. Only the senior leadership and century guards are allowed to possess weapons after curfew. A reminder, Team Two, centuries on duty are to be neutralized; we have been given the green light for them due to mission success calculations. Nothing we can do differently to avoid their removal; they have been deemed acceptable combatant losses. The last target for Montgomery and her team is the water tower; there, good old-fashioned satchel charges will be used. They will be placed to allow the tower to fall away from other buildings."

"Questions?" Krause asked, looking directly at the Delta that took Montgomery's right cross on his chin.

"Good, on to our final objective, three. We have learned that the components for manufacturing Ricin are located within the compound in building five, located in the most northeast portion of the compound."

Krause used the green laser to outline a circle around the building. "Which makes sense to keep it away from the rest of the population within the compound in case of an incident."

Krause turned to Kostas, "As soon as Wraith-Two breaches the chemical building's door, Alpha has the lead with Moore and Smith to set the charges. Montgomery on egress watch."

Giving Kostas a nod, Krause continued, "They know your style, I don't need you breaking in newbies tonight with that scary shit you deal with, like you had to do with Montgomery and me back in the Tajikistan in '03."

Kostas returned a single nod acknowledging his understanding.

This exchange got the young Delta's attention as he continued to rub his jaw and check for bleeding. Once satisfied that the bleeding had stopped, he looked at Montgomery and gave a nod of understanding with a 'my bad' expression, conceding that the 'old guy' was one to be respected.

"Per the plan Kostas laid out, Wraith-Two will breach the building with combat respirators on, document the materials with your helmet cams, then set the incendiary charges at a 3X factor."

Referring to three times the normal charges being set due to the need to neutralize the proteins of the Ricin Chain A and B components with extreme heat.

"We'll blow the chem building moments after we blow the food stores, water tower, and armory. A delayed detonation will be sequenced on the Ricin components, directly ensuring that the material will already be surrounded by high temperatures as it blows. Alpha will be giving a more comprehensive brief on building five and its contents after I conclude."

Again, a pause, "Drones will be live above the area of operation thirty minutes prior to entry at zero three hundred hours local. Our entry points are through the fences here and here, and egress the same. Montgomery's team with Alpha will enter at the fence closest to the chem building, and the rendition team here in the east. We will rendezvous at the LZ here at the abandoned elementary school, five miles to the north, here. You must be outside the fence by 04:15. The Big Blip will be deployed at 04:18. Precisely at 04:20, all charges will detonate, don't be running late team."

Krause paused, then continued, "ATF, FBI, Homeland Security, and local law enforcement will close the ring around the compound at exactly 04:30 to wait and highly encourage the occupants of the compound to surrender. Those agencies are counting on us for our part. All roads, trails, and paths will be secured to cut off any chances of escape. The folks in the compound will be left with no choice but an unarmed and unconditional surrender."

Krause surveyed the team with his gaze again, "Again, I remind you of General Morris's words, 'don't let this turn into some god damn Waco fucking Texas incident!'"

Chapter 51

The sound of gunfire overwhelmed the senses. Mary Rosenburg fell to the train car's floor, covering her young daughter as she looked up at the man in boots kneeling to remove something from his tool bag.

More gunfire came from the train's rear as it slowed near the next Station. Blood was running across the floor in front of Mary's face.

Matt Hudlebac rose from his crouched position next to his tool bag, in one hand he gripped tightly a small three-pound sledgehammer, in the other his Army-issued M7 bayonet.

He tossed the almost seven-inch-bladed knife to a man whom he did not know, who was sitting directly across from him on the train.

"Protect the woman and her child." Was all he said as he charged the first of the three gunmen who were dressed in suits and firing pistols at the southbound commuters.

Jack Flanagan caught the knife. Until that moment, Jack had been frozen in fear, still sitting upright in his seat.

Jack never served in the military, never even played a contact sport growing up. The closest to a physical confrontation he had ever come to was by way of a bully's punch to his gut in eighth grade.

Jack looked at the sheathed knife that he caught, completely bewildered and in a daze. He then looked at the woman and her daughter lying on the floor in pools of blood that were now running together. He blinked. When he opened his eyes, the woman lying on the floor was now his wife, Ann, the little girl she was shielding was his daughter, Bethany.

Something snapped in Jack at that moment, an emotional response that, if you asked anyone who knew him, they would have said he was incapable of. He removed the sheath from the knife and rose to follow the man in military boots and carrying a hammer.

Matt Hudlebac spent four years in the Army, almost half of that in Iraq and Afghanistan, as an infantry soldier. When he separated from the Army, he met his now husband John while using his GI Bill for his education at a Northern Virginia community college while receiving his HVAC certification, that he now used for his new career as a repair technician with a DC heating and air company.

Matt had witnessed and lived through horrible experiences while deployed. Those experiences taught him one hard lesson: inaction was a death sentence.

As he approached the first gunman who was attempting to reload, Matt threw the small sledgehammer with everything he had, striking the gunman square in the chest, incapacitating the gunman momentarily. As Matt fell onto the man, several bystanders, some with gunshot wounds, grabbed the arm and legs of the gunman. Matt pried the weapon from the gunman's hand, then he noticed his bayonet slide past his left eye and into the gunman's throat.

The other two gunman were directing their fire in the opposite direction of the train car. They did not see their murderous companion fall. In the chaos, they would have no clue that their end was near.

Matt, now on combat autopilot, dropped the magazine from the Colt 1911 pistol and replaced it with a full one from the now dead gunman's belt. Running out of rounds while engaged in a firefight was no longer a problem.

Matt gripped the Colt with both hands and started to advance toward the last two attackers, who were the only two people standing in the train car; everyone else was curled up into tight balls of weeping humanity or lying dead or injured on the floor.

Matt was now in his well-trained combat gait.

First his left foot, he placed the heel down, then rolled forward onto the toes. Then the right foot followed in a mirrored sequence, maintaining a slight bend in his knees, repeating the movement several times.

The attacker to his left, still not facing Matt, fell to his knees and then onto what was remaining of his face after the Colt's first shot passed through the back of his head, then out of the nasal cavity, removing most of his face except for his eyes.

The last remaining gunman looked shocked as he stared down at his now dead, well-dressed accomplice. As he turned to see Matt, the man's right eye disappeared as well as the back of his head when the Colt fired again.

Chapter 51

Krause started walking to the rear of the makeshift briefing room, "With no other questions for me, I'll let Alpha brief you on the Chem-Bio portion of objective two. Alpha."

As Kostas began to walk to the monitor, his phone buzzed; it was a text from Wade. "Another attack, this time the VRE, Zillinski's Tube Scenario."

Kostas looked at Krause, "We need to take five."

Krause nodded and, in a commanding voice, said, "Fiver, no more."

The Deltas began to disburse for either gear checks or bladder relief.

Kostas looked at Krause, "Follow me."

They found a rack compartment down the hall from the briefing room that was used for crew accommodations. As they entered the bunk area, Krause in a loud booming voice announced, "Everyone be somewhere else, now!"

None of the twelve or so US Naval personnel questioned the seasoned Delta; they quickly found somewhere else to be.

Kostas dialed Wade's number; he put it on speaker.

Wade answered on the first ring, "Mass casualty event, no info on the number of dead or wounded yet. Three shooters dressed as businessmen commuting home. One Army veteran and several bystanders took out all three gunmen. It would have been a lot worse if it weren't for them."

"Are we still green lit for this operation?" Kostas asked.

"Abso-fucking-lutly! Take those bastards down!" Was Wade's only reply, then Kostas hung up the phone.

"Do we let the teams know?" asked Krause.

"I don't see how we can keep it from them. It will be all over the ship soon if it isn't already. Besides, they're professionals, some of the best. Let's trust them to be professionals." Kostas replied.

Krause nodded.

Chapter 52

The dim light of the mission bay cast long shadows over the faces of the assembled teams. The air was thick with anticipation and the faint hum of the ship's engines. Kostas leaned back against the cold metal wall, internally reviewing the operation plan piece by piece. The plan was solid, but as with any operation, it was the execution that would make or break them.

"All right team," Krause said, projecting his authoritative voice. "Get your gear and double-check your packs. I want to see everyone ready to move in twenty minutes."

The teams dispersed in a controlled and silent flurry of activity. Kostas remained still for a moment, his mind running through the sequence of events that would unfold in the next few hours. He felt the familiar knot of tension in his gut, a constant companion before any mission. It wasn't fear; it was focus.

"Alpha, a word?" Krause's voice cut through his thoughts.

Kostas pushed off the wall and followed Krause to a quieter corner of the mission bay. Krause's face was etched with the lines of someone who had seen too much but couldn't afford to show it, a far stretch from the young man's face he had first met years ago.

"You've got the most critical part of this mission," Krause said, his voice low.

"In all things Chem-Bio and Nuke, I rely on you, always have. Will the charges neutralize the Ricin, or are we just hoping for the best?"

Kostas nodded. "I'm confident as long as the charges are sequenced correctly. Moore and Smith are solid; they were with us in '03 and '04, all over Afghanistan. They know how to follow my instructions to the letter. Besides, I've got Montgomery leading us," he said with a slight grin.

Krause gave a single curt nod and stepped back. "Good. Let's make this one clean."

Kostas nodded and moved on, satisfied. He found Moore and Smith performing buddy checks on their equipment.

"Ready?" Kostas asked, his voice carrying the weight of authority and experience.

Moore, a tall man with a shaved head and a perpetual scowl, nodded. "All set, Alpha."

Smith, a leaner, shorter, a more agile-looking soldier with sharp gray eyes, grinned. "Let's light up the night. Fourth of July in October"

Kostas allowed himself a small smile. "Just remember, no unnecessary risks. We're in and out, precise and clean."

They finished suiting up in silence, each movement practiced and efficient. The mission bay hummed with the sound of equipment shuffling and soldiers preparing for their mission.

Finally, Krause's voice cut through the noise, "Wraith-One and Two fall in!"

Both teams fell into a two-group formation, their faces masked in black with determination and focus. Krause stood before them, projecting confidence that Kostas knew was genuine.

"Remember your training, your past missions. Trust your team. Execute the plan. And above all, keep your heads. We're not here to play hero. We're here to complete a mission."

A chorus of affirmations followed, and with a final nod, Krause led them to the deployment area. The Littoral's rear flight deck opened to the night, the cool lake air a sharp contrast to the warmth of the ship's interior.

The teams boarded each of the waiting MH-60M Black Hawks in sequence according to the team assignments. The tension palpable as each Black Hawk touched down, then slightly hovered over the deck of the helipad of the Littoral one at a time. Then each taking off into the night.

Kostas found his seat, the familiar hum of the rotors filling his ears. He began to box breathe silently. Then, he glanced and nodded at Moore and Smith, both were focused and ready.

"Let's do this," Kostas muttered, more to himself than anyone else.

The helicopters disappeared into the night, the dark waters of Lake Superior below them as they rode in silence. The drop zone was less than ten miles away now, and every second brought them closer to the execution of yet another WMD worst-case scenario. Kostas closed his eyes, running through the plan one last time.

The radio crackled to life. "Five minutes out," the Black Hawk pilot announced.

Kostas opened his eyes and looked around the cabin. Faces still set in grim determination met his gaze.

"Two minutes!" the pilot called.

Kostas tightened his grip on his weapon with his right hand, then with his left, giving the ammo magazine a slap. His heart rate steady. Like an old friend, he felt the adrenaline coursing through his veins, sharpening his senses. Once again, this was it.

The helicopters hovered just above a small grove of thinned-out treetops, then ropes were deployed from both Black Hawks. One by one, the Deltas descended into the darkness, their movements swift and silent. Kostas hit the ground and immediately scanned the area with his NODS, or Night Optical Device. Wraith-Two fell into position around Montgomery, Wraith-One around Krause.

"Wraith-Two, move out," Montgomery whispered into her comm.

They advanced on their silent e-bikes toward the breach point fence, the night enveloping them.

Moore cut through the chain-link with practiced ease, and they slipped through the gap, their movements fluid without the smallest error. The compound campus loomed ahead, dark silhouettes against the night sky.

Wraith-Two made their way to building five, the chemical manufacturing facility.

Montgomery ordered the team to don their respirators. Then with a nod and a quiet "Go." Smith defeated the lock.

The chemical building's door gave way with a soft click as Smith disabled the lock, then they were inside.

The air was thick with the scent of chemicals. Kostas's NODs gave him clear eyesight of the components stored within the room, his helmet-mounted camera documenting everything. Montgomery now functioned as the rear guard protecting their egress from the small building. The rest of the team carried the incendiary charges while documenting the stockpile of containers and equipment.

Kostas keyed his mic, "Moore, double that charge in the northeast corner near the three barrels over there. The way everything is stored in here requires a slight adjustment in the charge location."

Moore only said, "WILCO." Then got to the task.

"Charges set," Moore reported to Montgomery.

Kostas checked his watch. *We're on schedule.* He thought to himself.

Montgomery's voice came across the comms, "Wraith-Two, let's move."

They exited the building in single coverage, leaving behind a network of incendiary devices. As they regrouped outside the breached door, the compound remained silent. The rest of the Deltas were in position, ready to execute their parts of the mission.

"Wraith-One, this is Wraith-Two," Montgomery whispered into her comm. "Phase one complete. Preparing for phase two."

Krause glanced behind his shoulder at the rest of Wraith-One, giving the team a thumbs up. In less than twenty minutes, most of the compound would be a smoldering ruin, and the threat of Ricin would be neutralized. Time to secure the human targets.

Kostas took a deep breath, the night air filling his lungs. The mission was far from over, but the most critical part was done. Now, it was a matter of precision and timing.

To himself, Krause muttered, "Let's finish this."

Chapter 53

August 2003, Pamir Mountains

Captain Kostas Papadopoulos crouched behind a rocky outcrop, scanning the desolate landscape with his optics.

At this elevation in the Pamir Mountains near Tajikistan, the temperature was stuck at fifty-five degrees, starkly contrasting to the rest of the AOR in the lowlands of Afghanistan this time of year.

The sun dipped behind the mountain range, casting long shadows over the terrain of the border region in Afghanistan. Temperatures will start to fall.

As Kostas sat in the shadows with the team comprised of four members of a Combat Control Team or CCT that were already in the area, orchestrating bombing missions of bunker-busting bombs.

Rounding out the hastily cobbled-together team was a single Pararescueman or PJ who served as a medic. Kostas tried to impress the danger and magnitude of the suspected Ricin chemical components to the deadly air traffic controllers of forward combat.

Now they were an impromptu hostage recovery force, due to the logistics of the mountainous region and the zero availability of a SEAL or Delta teams this far north in the window of time they had for the rescue.

Waiting for additional SOF units was off the table due to Intel's timeline for the projected Ricin experiment. It was up to these six to recover the hostage and document the chemical manufacturing capabilities and then call in an airstrike to destroy the cave and all that it contained.

To Kostas's left, Senior Airman Tom Krause, the youngest CCT member in the group, looked like he was going to vomit after hearing Kostas describe the slow process of certain death by Ricin exposure.

To his right knelt Master Sergeant Hurley, the team lead. Kostas may outrank everyone on this team; however, he knew his business—chemical weapons, not tactical operations.

He let Hurley command and signaled this to the entire team by removing his rank insignia from his uniform.

The mission was clear but dangerous; time was running out for the captive Airman.

Three weeks earlier, Air Force Airman Dawn Montgomery, a communications specialist, had been taken hostage after a convoy attack outside Kabul. Intel reports from a nearby village confirmed the presence of a female US military hostage in a cave guarded by Al-Qaeda fighters who were collaborating with the Islamic Movement of Uzbekistan or IMU to develop chemical weapons.

Additional intel reports pointed to Montgomery being a test subject to determine the lethality of the manufactured weapons, and it would likely be recorded not only for perfecting their deadly craft but also for propaganda material.

Kostas glanced at Tom. "Ready?"

Krause nodded; his face set, but pale and determined. "Let's get her back."

Hurley gave one last brief, covering everyone's roles. Kostas would be the second-to-last to enter the cave. The PJ, who was also combat trained well beyond Kostas, would serve at the rear.

The team moved swiftly and silently, advancing toward the cave entrance. Krause took point, his sharp eyes scanning for any signs of movement through his NODs. The rest of the CCT members followed closely, weapons at the ready. As they approached the narrow cave entrance, Krause signaled for the assaulters to enter. The path was dark and increasingly narrow as they continued. They could hear muffled voices echoing from within.

Hurley asked in a whisper, "Where is a linguist when you need one?"

Kostas returned the whisper, "Does it matter what they are saying at this point?"

"No."

Kostas nodded.

The path opened and slowly became wider, but in a downward direction. Without their night vision, they would have fallen down hopelessly the slick stone slope.

Krause signaled to stop and get low, his M4 at the ready. Kostas couldn't tell if the voices were in front of them or behind due to the echoing.

There was a small light hanging from a wire at a fork in the cave. Before them, two tunnels, one small, one slightly larger. Hurley motioned to divide into two groups of three. The four CCTs would split and take one tag along at each of their rears.

With a deep breath, Kostas followed Krause and other combat controller into the smaller tunnel, his weapon ready. Silently hoping that they would not need the medical training or the combat expertise of the PJ who went with Hurley's group.

The air increasingly became cooler and damper as they continued down the tunnel, the hum of what seemed to be a generator rumbled and echoed on the walls of the cave. The scent of stale mildew filled his nostrils, then the distinct sweet chemical smell that Kostas immediately recognized as Triton X-100, a surfactant used in Ricin manufacturing. A nonionic substance by itself, it was often used for protein extraction and solubilization of Ricin.

As the two controllers checked their six o'clock position, Kostas signaled to stop, then slowly started backing up and motioned for the other two to follow. Kostas led them back to a bend in the tunnel where he felt he could communicate with Krause and the other controller Reynolds.

He whispered, "We're close to the chemical manufacturing area. That sweet smell is Triton, it's used in Ricin manufacturing."

The two combat controllers looked like they were told they had just inhaled poison. "Don't worry, by itself, it is mostly harmless, but it means we are close. Don your respirators."

They did with hurried efficiency.

As the three continued past the point where they turned around, the sound of echoing gunfire filled the air.

"Is it in front of us or behind? I can't tell." Kostas asked.

"It has to be Hurley and his team," Krause replied. "Get ready."

As the words left his respirator, the radio crackled with difficulty in this cave, "…contact...Hurley… bleeding bad…PJ KIA…Tangos down…" Then the radio went silent.

Not missing a beat, Krause signaled to quickly move forward, past another turn, where the glow of light was present, and yelling voices. They removed their NODs and moved forward rapidly. Before Kostas even registered the sound of the shot, he felt a shocking hammer blow to his weapon, staggering him back. All hell broke loose.

Krause opened fire while Reynolds laid down cover fire. Kostas got down on the floor of the tunnel and hugged the inner wall of the turn.

Reynolds yelled, "Alphabet, get up here and lay down cover fire!"

As Kostas reached a spot to fire from, his weapon did nothing after he pulled the trigger. He rolled the M4 over to see a bullet hole in the lower receiver just above the trigger guard.

The weapon now rendered useless, Kostas cast the lifesaving, but now worthless rifle across the cave and pulled his Beretta M9 from the holster at his thigh.

"Alphabet, get up here!" It was Krause.

There was no mistaking that Krause was yelling for him. Just as Reynolds had done, instead of trying to remember the name Papadopoulos, they had improvised.

Kostas quickly advanced, his M9 leading the way.

Kostas walked into a large, well-lit room with tables, chairs, and laboratory equipment scattered everywhere.

"Where's your M4?" Reynolds asked as he bandaged Krause's left leg right above the knee.

"Is he all right?" Kostas asked.
Krause answered, "I'm fine, 'tis a flesh wound." Then he laughed. "What is all of this?"

"Part of what we came for. By first look, it hasn't been weaponized yet." Replied Kostas as he removed his respirator after checking his handheld ion spectrometer that is used to take air samples.

"How do you know?" asked Krause.

Kostas shook the device in the air in front of him. "This and those guys you killed aren't wearing any PPE to protect themselves. Do we go after Hurley's team?"

"That's your call, Alphabet. You're the Chem-Bio expert. This is one of our two primary objectives." Krause replied, agitated with the situation.

Reynolds spoke up, "Did you hear that?"

"What?" Krause said.

"Listen."

A small voice repeated, "Hello?" It was faint, but it was a woman's voice. "I'm an American, Airman First Class Montgomery."

Krause immediately readied his weapon, as did Reynolds. Krause said, "Lie down on your stomach, arms stretched out. We will secure you soon. Are you injured?"

"No. I know what to do. I had HRC training when I arrived in the country."

HRC, or High-Risk Capture training, is a requirement once military personnel arrive in a combat zone. It is designed to prepare individuals who may be at risk of being kidnapped, taken hostage, or captured, especially in hostile or austere environments.

"That's good, Airman Montgomery. Then we will keep the comms minimal until we get there. Can you walk?"

"I can run if you give me the opportunity."

Krause smiled and whispered, "She's got spunk." Then, into the tunnel, he said, "Any tangos?"

"How many did you kill?" the voice asked.

"Five."

"Then be on the lookout for five more."

"Copy," Krause said with a grim nod.

Kostas started looking everywhere, worried that the combat wasn't over and his M$ was useless.

Krause turned and said to Kostas and Reynolds, "On to objective two."

Once again, facing down the other tunnel, M4 at the ready, Krause said, "Airman Montgomery, remember the game Marco Polo when you were a kid?"

Sounding a bit confused, her echo replied, "Yes?"

"Good, that's what we are going to play while we look for tangos and you. Any tangos near you?"

"No."

"Good, remember your training. Now, let's play… Marco."

"Polo." She replied.

Krause turned to Kostas and said, "Alpha, do your thing. We will be back soon. You might want to grab one of those AKs on the floor since your M4 is gone."

Kostas nodded, retrieved an AK-47 from next to one of the dead, and pulled the bolt back on the unfamiliar weapon.

"Reynolds give him a thirty-second tutorial," Krause said.

Taking the weapon from Kostas, Reynolds picked up an extra magazine then briefly showed Kostas how to load and unload the magazine from the rifle, then handed it back. "Give me the extra mags for your M4, put these in their place. It's on full auto, spray and pray if you have to."

Kostas nodded and complied after holstering his M9 Beretta.

"We may have to make Alpha an honorary Air Commando," Krause said while smiling.

Kostas thought to himself, *at least it's no longer Alphabet.*

Then, the two men advanced down the unexplored tunnel, weapons ready. Leaving Kostas alone to document the lab.

"Marco…Polo," came the distinct echoes of Krause and Montgomery.

Kostas slung the AK over his shoulder, then got to work documenting and identifying the chemical components in the storage cabinets and shelves.

As he took photos of everything with his right hand, he held the ion sensor in his left. Shaking his head, he thought to himself, *I don't know how those two cleared this room without putting a round through any of this. Thanks for small favors and good marksmanship!*

The echo of 'Marco' came to his ears, then gunfire erupted.

As Kostas unslung the AK from his shoulder, dropping both the camera and the sensor, an enemy fighter emerged from the tunnel where both Krause and Reynolds disappeared into.

As he pulled the trigger on the AK-47, the recoil and violence of the fully automatic fire startled him as he sprayed the bearded man and the wall behind him.

The mag was now empty, which only took a few seconds.

Kostas fumbled with the mag release latch, trying frantically to reload the weapon, worried that another tango would emerge from the tunnel.

"Polo?" came the faint and quizzical female echo.

"Four tangos down." Came the echo of Krause's voice.

Without thinking, Kostas replied, "One tango down."

"Good, that makes five. Keep your head on a swivel, Alpha," came Krause's reply from the dark void.

"Copy." Kostas continued to fumble with the magazine, failing miserably at the reloading effort. Finally, as the three figures emerged from the tunnel, Kostas abandoned the AK and drew his M9 again.

"Marco," came Krause's voice with a smile. Reynolds was covering their rear, Airman Dawn Montgomery was in between them, still in her ACU uniform, looking dirty but overall healthy. Evidently, killing her with Ricin in uniform was important to these bastards.

"Polo," Kostas replied and holstered his weapon. "Couldn't reload the AK?"

In a sheepish growl, Kostas grudgingly admitted, "No."

"Here, I'll show you again. Nice work, by the way, Alpha. You're now an honorary Air Commando. Forgive us; the formal ceremony will have to wait."

Krause reloaded the AK for Kostas and then asked, "Is your work with the Ricin components done here?"

Kostas nodded.

"Ricin?" Airman Dawn Montgomery spoke for the first time.

Turning serious, Krause said, "Alpha can scare the shit out of you later with his tutorial on Ricin, for now we have got to make contact with Hurley's team. No one gets left behind. Alpha escort Airman Montgomery back out of the cave, see if you can get comms back to CC." referring to Centralized Command.

"Give them status and get evac on the way. Reynolds and I are going after the others."

"Can I get a rifle?" asked Montgomery.

"Sorry, no. Not part of the SOPs in an operation like this." Krause replied. "Now let's move."

As the team of now four made their way to the main tunnel, Krause and Reynolds led the way with their NODs. Both Reynolds and Krause saluted Kostas as they parted and made their way toward Master Sergeant Hurley's team.

"Follow me, keep one hand on my belt, stick to me like glue. It's going to be dark and slick the rest of the way." Kostas instructed Montgomery as he pulled his M9 to her and handed it butt first.

"Here. If you shoot one of our friendlies, those two will shoot me and remove my title as honorary Air Commando. Remember your training, don't fire randomly.

She nodded and said, "Thank you, I feel better now."

He nodded and started up the slick slope.

When they reached the entrance to the cave, Kostas instructed Montgomery on the agreed upon call signs to radio in their status and request evac with medical.

"You're Comms, right?" He asked, she nodded.

"Good, get back in your communication specialist saddle, and let CC know we are ready for evac. I will cover you."

"What shall I say is the other team's status?" she asked.

"Unknown at this time."

She nodded and got to work.

As she finished, a crackle came over the radio, "Alpha?" It was Krause's voice.

Montgomery replied, "Go for Alpha."

"On the way up the slope, two KIA, one needs medical evac."

"Team Alpha copies, will update CC momentarily."

Kostas looked at her through his NODs, "Team Alpha?"

She smiled, "Seemed appropriate." Then she gave the update to Centralized Command.

"Copy Team Alpha. Two dark birds in the air, ETA under twenty. We have two hot loads en route to do some house cleaning for you. You're coming home Team Alpha."

"Team Alpha out, for now," she spoke into the radio.

"Hey, what is your real name, Alpha?"

"Kostas, Kostas Papadopoulos."

She smiled again, "We'll stick with Alpha."

As they loaded the wounded Master Sergeant in the first UH-60 helicopter, Krause handed Montgomery an M4 rifle. "Here, it will serve you better than Alpha's M9, cover us while we recover the dead and get them loaded."

With beaming pride, she took the rifle and took cover behind a rock, looking like a seasoned operator with Kostas's night vision optics on her head.

That was the defining moment in Dawn Montgomery's life and career.

Instead of leaving the Air Force after the killing of the members of her convoy and being released from her over three-week captivity, she made one request. To transfer into the Air Force's Intel community.

Later, that career move would allow her to apply, with Krause's recommendation, to join the 1st Special Forces Operational Detachment-Delta as one of the rare females who dared.

"All right, Alpha, this is it. Good luck." Krause said as he stuck out a hand.

"You're not coming?"

"Someone has to stay behind and laser paint that entrance for the inbound F-16s to drop the bombs that will blow that cave and everything in it to hell. Reynolds and I will make sure it happens. This is what we do." He smiled.

Then added, "Take care of Montgomery and don't forget to put your rank back on your shirt, Captain."

Then, with a laugh, he said, "Oh, and if you ever need a refresher on how to reload an AK-47, just let me know."

Chapter 56

Kostas scanned the area of the compound within view of his NODs, every sense heightened. The night was silent, but the weight of what was to come hung in the air. Both Teams were now in their next positions, waiting for the signal to move. He checked his watch again, the seconds ticking down to the critical moment.

"Wraith-Two, maintain visuals on targets, provide tango support as necessary after placing the rest of your charges." Krause's voice came over the comm.

"Montgomery, you're clear to proceed."

Montgomery's team moved again with practiced precision, slipping through the shadows toward the dining facility and armory. Kostas was now at the rear of Wraith-Two.

These two teams comprised some of the best operators in the world; they meticulously planned for every contingency, but even the best plans could go awry once the operational die was cast.

As Montgomery's team approached the dining facility and food storage building, a sudden movement caught her eye. She raised her hand, signaling the team to hold. Through her scope, she watched a guard emerging from a building, a cigarette glowing red in the dark.

"Hold position," She whispered into the comm. "We have a sentry near building seven."

The team froze after melting into the shadows. The guard took a few puffs of the cigarette, glancing around the dark compound. Time seemed to stretch as seconds felt like minutes while they waited for him to move on.

To Kostas's left, he could see Montgomery's finger hovering next to the trigger, ready to take the shot if necessary.

Finally, the guard flicked the cigarette away and turned back toward the building.

"Proceed," she said softly, removing her finger from the trigger guard and placing it in parallel to the weapon's barrel again, firmly on the lower receiver.

Wraith-Two resumed their advance, reaching the dining facility's entrance. They moved with silent efficiency as top-of-the-food-chain predators moved through tall grass in the night, setting the charges with swift, precise movements.

Kostas shifted his focus to securing their exit, ensuring there were no unfriendlies about.

"Wraith-One, Wraith-Two; charges set at first two buildings," Montgomery reported. "Moving to the armory, then water tower."

"Copy that, Wraith-Two," Krause replied.

Chapter 55

"Wraith-One, moving to Objective One," Krause whispered into his comm.

The team advanced through the gap, their movements ghost-like on their electronic bikes with a single-wheeled mobile medical litter trailing behind each bike. They approached the two-story apartment building housing the militia leaders and their families. Krause gave a quick hand signal, and the team took their positions around the entrances.

"Gas ready?" Krause asked.

"Ready," one of the team members replied, removing the four canisters, the size of small propane bottles used for camping lanterns from his pack. He distributed them among the team.

"Don your respirators," Krause said as he pulled his over his mouth.

As the team moved to their positions covering the exits on each level of the apartment building, Krause's voice once again was in all their earpieces, "Deploy on my mark. Three, two, one, mark."

The canisters were released, a soft hiss filled the air as the knockout gas spread from each end of the hallways on both the top and ground level floors.

All the members of Wraith-One started banging on doors and yelling, "FIRE, FIRE! EXIT OUT THE STAIRS, QUICKLY!"

As apartment room doors began to open with panicked and bewildered people, one by one, they hit the floor as the HVAC system spread the gas throughout the building.

Krause led the way through the ground level floor, his weapon at the ready, providing cover for his team as they moved through the rooms with practiced efficiency, securing first the rooms, then the incapacitated targets, their wrists quickly bound with zip ties.

"Wraith-Two, this is Wraith-One. Targets are secure." Krause reported while watching one of the militiamen being loaded onto a mobile litter.

The process was repeated for each of the other found targets. Each bound and hooded prisoner was searched thoroughly, and anything that could be used as a weapon and any useful intel was confiscated. Krause's earlier words echoed once again across the comms: "No lethality unless absolutely necessary."

The team moved swiftly but carefully, ensuring no unnecessary harm came to the noncombatants. As they exited the building, they regrouped outside, their mission almost complete.

Now to transport the targets beyond the fence and to the LZ.

Chapter 56

The tension in the air was palpable as they waited for the final confirmation. Krause's steady and calm voice came over the comm.

Kostas's grip tightened on his weapon. He watched as Montgomery's team reached the water tower, placing the last of the charges.

"Objective Two secure," Montgomery confirmed, "We're moving to egress."

"Copy that," Krause said. "Wraith-One, begin extraction. All teams, stand by for detonation."

Mongomery said, "Let's move."

Kostas nodded, then they began their own silent retreat toward the fence. Every step was measured, every sound muffled by the night as they increased their distance from the chemical building. As they reached the breach point, Kostas glanced back at the compound. In a few minutes, it would be unrecognizable.

"The Big Blip is live," Krause announced, "Detonation in two minutes."

Kostas and his team slipped through the fence, moving quickly but cautiously toward their waiting electronic bikes that were placed several yards off the main trail.

As they rode the bicycles in silence, navigating still with their night vision, the abandoned elementary school loomed quietly in the distance.

Wraith-Two was now clear of the fence before the EMP and subsequent explosions rendered the compound a smoking ruin.

"Wraith-Two, approaching LZ," Montgomery reported, "We're on schedule."

"Copy that," Krause replied.

"Wraith-One, clear of the egress point, we are out of the fence. All tangos are secure except for the king of clubs and the king of diamonds."

Referring to Lawrence and Red and their card deck designators.

"Both kings were not on the table." Now, referring to the mission landscape as the playing table.

"All units, prepare for EMP."

As the school came closer into view through the night vision NODs, Wraith-Two ducked into the shadows to wait.

The night was still, and the tension was thick enough to cut with a knife. Kostas checked his watch, counting down the seconds.

"Big Blip in five, four, three, two, one…" came Krause's voice over the earpiece.

An invisible but powerful pulse rippled silently through the air and power lines. The lights still on in the compound flickered briefly, then died, plunging the targeted area into the surrounding darkness.

A few heartbeats later, the first explosion rocked the night, followed by a series of detonations that lit up the sky fractions of a second later.

Kostas watched the glow emerging from over the treetops as the chemical building, the dining facility, and the armory were consumed in almost simultaneous flames. He knew the compound would now be a scene of chaos, smoke billowing into the sky from the bright flames on the ground.

The mission was a success.

"Detonations confirmed," Krause said, his voice barely audible over the roar of the explosions, "All Wraiths, proceed to final egress."

Kostas motioned to his team, and they moved quickly toward the waiting Black Hawks. The helicopters descended like dark angels, their rotors whipping the air into a frenzy. Kostas and Wraith-Two boarded swiftly, as the birds hovered less than eighteen inches over the ground, then lifted off.

As they ascended, Kostas looked down at the burning compound as he breathed. The job was done, but the night was far from over. They had neutralized the threat, but the aftermath would be dealt with by others.

"Good work, Alpha," Krause said, clapping Kostas on the shoulder, "Let's get back and debrief."

Kostas nodded, the adrenaline slowly ebbing away. He leaned back in his seat, closing his eyes for a moment. The mission had been a success, but they were missing the two kings.

"Homeward bound," the pilot announced.

The Black Hawks turned toward the horizon, carrying the team away from the chaos they had created. Kostas opened his eyes, the first light of dawn beginning to break. The world below was still, as the firelight faded into the distance.

Chapter 57

FOR IMMEDIATE RELEASE

Title: Successful Overnight Raid on Domestic Terrorist Compound in Upper Peninsula, Michigan

Subhead: Suspected Terrorist Raid Linked to VRE Massacre

Date: October 2, 2024

By: Nunzio Vittone for NPR News

NEWBERRY, MI - In a decisive overnight operation, a joint force of state, local, and federal agencies successfully raided a domestic terrorist compound in the Upper Peninsula of Michigan. The raid follows the tragic attack on the Virginia Railway Express (VRE) from Washington, DC to Fredericksburg during yesterday afternoon's commuter rush.

At approximately 3:00 a.m. today, a coordinated assault was launched on a known militia compound suspected of harboring and manufacturing deadly Ricin. This action comes in response to anonymous tips received about the group's intentions and capabilities following yesterday's attack on the VRE in Virginia that left dozens dead and more wounded. The urgency of the raid was heightened by the need to neutralize the Ricin threat promptly.

The joint force, comprised of Homeland Security, the Michigan State Police, and other federal agencies, executed the operation with precision. There were no casualties reported among the raiding teams or the compound's occupants. Several buildings within the compound were destroyed, and large fires were still burning as dawn broke.

In a joint press conference held earlier this morning by Homeland Security and the Michigan State Police, officials confirmed that all members of the militia group are surrendering and cooperating with authorities. The swift and cooperative response of the terrorists is seen as a significant step toward ensuring public safety.

DoD chemical warfare experts, who served as an advisory part of the operation, confirmed that all components of Ricin found within the compound have been neutralized and destroyed. This swift action eliminates the immediate threat posed by the terrorists' capabilities to produce and deploy this deadly substance here in the United States.

Homeland Security Secretary Janet Walker praised the operation's success, stating, "The swift and coordinated efforts of our state, local, and federal partners have averted yet another potentially catastrophic event. We will continue to work diligently to protect our nation from such threats."

Michigan State Police Commissioner James Thompson added, "This raid demonstrates the effectiveness of inter-agency cooperation. We are grateful for the bravery and professionalism displayed by all personnel involved."

President Adams is scheduled to provide an updated statement from the White House within the hour, addressing the nation on the operation and further steps being taken to ensure national security.

For further details, please contact:
Office of Public Affairs
Homeland Security
Phone: 1-800-123-4567
Email: publicaffairs@dhs.gov

Michigan State Police Public Information Office
Phone: 1-800-555-5555
Email: publicinfo@michiganpolice.gov

Chapter 58

With both Lawrence and Red not being found at the compound and the railway attack in Virginia, Kostas felt that something else was afoot. As he entered the plane's SCIF and prepared to take off from Marquette Sawyer Regional Airport, he called Hogan's cell. "I would like to talk, actually, Katherine, I would like to listen."

There was a long pause then, Hogan replied, "Where?"

Kostas replied, "Richmond, The Jefferson Hotel. It's not the Little Inn at Washington, but it still has a bed and good food. I'll make the reservation."

She asked, "When?"

"Tomorrow night too soon? Say seven p.m. for dinner and drinks at Lemaire on the lobby floor?"

"I'm familiar with it," she said cautiously.

With a little portrayed enthusiasm, he said, "Great, I look forward to listening more to you and whatever else may arise."

She hung up.

He next dialed Jess, "Ready for some overwatch?"

Referring to the tactical practice of having a team member in a position to observe and provide protective fire if needed from a sniper's position.

"Please tell me it's the redhead," she replied with ice in her tone.

"Consider it your Christmas bonus, Jess." He clicked off.

Chapter 59

Jess made the dinner reservations for Kostas and Hogan at Lemaire for six thirty, that extra time would give Kostas a chance to evaluate the situation and ensure there was no one else looking to crash the party. Both agreed that Hogan would also be showing up earlier than the seven o'clock agreed upon time. While Kostas was in the restaurant with Hogan, Jess would have limited visibility of the situation in the room.

Jess showed up in person at The Jefferson to make the reservations in person and perform a site survey of the restaurant and hotel room, as well as all entrance and exit points.

Requests like this were not unusual for the hotel or the restaurants within The Jefferson; many politicians and high-power executives stayed and dined at the historic hotel in downtown Richmond.

Security teams frequently practiced the same protocols as Jess did, however, when Jess insisted on a window table, the hotel's manager was surprised. "Oh… typically our visiting VIPs request interior rooms and tables."

Jess smiled sweetly and replied, "This one will be fine; besides, it has a nice view." I

t had no view, just the sidewalk and traffic on Franklin Street. Still, Jess used the opportunity to sit in one of the chairs and appeared to gaze out the window, when in reality she was expertly attaching a small listening device to the underside of the table.

Not wanting to offend or be disagreeable to the customer, the manager smiled back and replied, "Perfect, I'll lock it down for your party. Would you like to see the room now?"

Jess looked up and replied, "That would be lovely, thank you." As they entered the suite directly across from the apartment that Jess secured across the street, the manager stood pleasantly in the door as Jess walked around the two-room suite.

Jess turned to her, "Do you mind if I take a few photos? My boss is a detail-oriented kind of guy; he likes to know that everything is up to his standard."

"Please, by all means, take as many as you like."

Jess used her phone not only to take photos from multiple angles in the room but also to capture the view from outside the bedroom window. As she continued throughout the suite, she also attached several listening devices in strategic locations, including the bedroom.

"Thank you so much for the tour, this will be perfect," Jess said pleasantly to the manager.

As Jess exited The Jefferson Hotel, she walked past the valet and fountain, then crossed the street mid-block and walked into the fourteen-story apartment building. Once she arrived at the door of the apartment, she did not need a key. It was unlocked. Kostas was standing next to a shooter's tripod and staring out at the hotel room Jess had just left.

"Comms-check good?" she asked.

"Five by five." Came Kostas's response, "Great job Jess."

"Shooting lanes as we expected?"

Kostas replied, "Yes, as you expected. You're the master planner, remember?"

"Thanks, boss." She winked.

"On that note. What's this whole thing? Your boss is a detail kind of guy; he likes to know that everything is up to his standard." He laughed, "I may be all of that to a certain extent, but you trump me in spades in the details and standards department."

She laughed, "Tess teases me on that also. Old Army habit."

Kostas turned back to the window and the view of the table for two below, "The only issue will be the line of sight in the restaurant; however, you knew that would be the case. You will only be able to see the table and the two of us in the chairs, not the entire room from this elevated position."

"Right, it won't be a problem with the rest of the MGSI security detail. Act one for the night should be relatively calm, I suggest you get the herb roasted halibut or the mushroom casarecce with a nice white wine and enjoy it because act two may not be enjoyable at all."

Kostas gave a grim nod.

Chapter 60

Kostas sat at the table for two with a smoked old-fashioned complete with a large ice cube and two Luxardo cherries, the menu called it a Phoenix Feather.

His phone vibrated, he looked at the screen without picking it up. Jess's text read "The analyst's report is in."

This was a predetermined set of codes that Jess and Kostas agreed upon to ensure Kostas received timely intel concerning the situation on the ground, but not raise Hogan's suspicions if she happened to glance at the phone's screen. Both Jess and Kostas agreed that the use of an earwig was out of the question, she would be looking for it.

The 'analyst' referred to Hogan, and the word 'in' meant she was now in the restaurant. As anticipated, Hogan had shown up an hour early.

MGSI's surveillance team was milling about the restaurants and the hotel lobby disguised as patrons on dates or on business meetings.

From her elevated perch behind the FN SCAR-17S sniper rifle, resting in the tripod across the street, Jess was the communication hub. The NightForce scope attached to the Picatinny rail provided all the optics she needed to monitor everything.

Through the scope, she could even see that one of the Luxardo cherries in Kostas's drink was missing its stem, but not the other.

In reply to Jess's text, he tapped his right index finger on the drink's rim. Also, a predetermined code.

Hogan appeared from the bar area, which was in the adjacent room to the one Kostas was seated in. She was dressed to the nines to say the least, the shoes alone had to be well out of her salary range. The dress was long and black, cut low and emphasized the attractive curves of her fit body. The dress created a wicked contrast with her red hair, which was now worn down instead of her normal FBI regulation style. The color black meeting the red at her shoulders set an image of lava overtaking night. She smiled, he stood and returned the smile, then leaned in for a brief embrace and a kiss on her cheek. She returned the kiss, but on his lips.

He did his best to fake a convincing smile, then pulled her chair out for her.

She sat and said, "Well, I guess this qualifies for you buying me dinner, we'll see if a marriage offer is in order at some other time."

Kostas again forced a smile and said, "Ahh, your interrogation of me back at General Morris's office. Only time will tell."

He sat down, still forcing a small chuckle.

"I see you started without me." She nodded at the old-fashioned on the table.

"Wasn't sure if you would be fashionably late." He replied. Then his phone vibrated, and both looked at the screen that was intentionally left visible on the table.

The text read, "I hope this analyst gives me a reason to terminate her, I am already tired of her shit."

"HR issues? Employee problems?" Hogan asked.

"Always. Curse of the executive life." Kostas said with a grimace while he tapped his glass rim, feeling his skin crawl. He got the attention of the server and asked Hogan what she would like to start with.

"I'll have the same as the gentlemen."

"Very well, ma'am." The server replied and then made her way to the bar.

Hogan broke the silence, "So you said you want to listen?"

"Yes, it seemed our last meal together never got to a point that you may have been driving at, and I didn't see it at the time.

Admittedly, I may have been a little short-sighted not taking you up on working closer together."

Hogan's eyebrows raised, "I see." She paused, seeming to make a mental calculation and plan her next words carefully. "Does General Morris know we are meeting?"

"In a roundabout way, yes. The details are on a need to know basis."

She smiled as her drink arrived, but her eyes never left Kostas's. "You know the great thing about cherries are the stems."

"The stems? I don't understand."

"Gives me an opportunity to demonstrate a skill, with the right audience, which I think I have."

"A skill?"

"I'll demonstrate." Hogan took one of the cherries from her glass and slowly placed it on her red lips, then opened her mouth, and both the stem and the cherry disappeared into her smile. Then with what seemed little effort, she swallowed, paused, and then removed the stem from her mouth, which was now tied into a knot.

"It's all in the tongue; a talented tongue can accomplish a lot."

Kostas feigned interest, "I like talented partners."

He had seen this bar trick before and thought it was tacky and for college kids. She didn't realize it had the exact opposite effect on him than she intended.

He smiled and gave a single nod as if to appreciate it while thinking to himself, Jess might pull the trigger after that stunt. Either that or vomit.

The server returned, "Can I tell you about the specials the chef has prepared for tonight?"

"Still locking eyes with Kostas, Hogan said, "No thanks, I already know what I want."

Emphasizing the last three words. Kostas was sure a 7.62 round would be coming through the window any second.

The server blushed a little, but Kostas kept his composure and smiled back at Hogan to acknowledge that the message had been received.

He then said, "I heard the halibut is good."

Hogan cooed, "Perfect."

His phone vibrated, Jess's text read "This analyst is really pissing me off, can I get rid of her?"

He tapped the rim of his now empty glass twice, signaling a negative response, and smiled.

"We'll both have the herb roasted halibut please, and a bottle of the Alphonse Mellot "La Moussiere" Sancerre '20, please, not the '21. I believe its bin 103."

"Very good, Sir." Replied the server, now wanting to run away from the table.

Good to get the server out of the path of any brain matter that might get splattered if Jess loses her patience with Hogan, he thought to himself while smiling.

"Do you need to address those messages?" Hogan asked with a smile.

"No, nothing that can't wait until later." He replied.

He then felt her foot slowly work its way up the inside of his leg, then the server returned with the bottle of wine.

"Sir." Presenting the cork to him after removing it from the bottle.

The server poured a sample of the wine for Kostas and waited for his approval; he nodded. As the wine was poured for each of them, they toasted, and then the server returned the bottle to the chiller on the table.

Hogan asked, "So Wade doesn't know about the circumstances of our meeting tonight?"

Kostas thought to himself, *she said Wade, not General Morris.*

"No, no, he just knows that I planned on speaking to you to collaborate further, especially since Lawrence and Red were nowhere to be found after the raid in Michigan and the attack on the VRE."

Her demeanor shifted at the mention of the two names.

"I'm sure they will turn up." She said dismissively, and for the first time since she sat down, her eyes moved away from his.

He sipped his wine, then returned the glass to the table. "The FBI have any leads on where they are at or where they went?"

She now looked bored, "We have Red on traffic cams off the Ohio and Pennsylvania Turnpikes and at toll gates in the DC Metro area. Lawrence disappeared without a trace."

She smiled, then her demeanor shifted and brightened just as quickly as it dimmed, as she found a way to shift the conversation.

"Hey, I thought you wanted to listen? That means I do more of the talking, no questions from you." She said with her best sultry red smile she could manage.

He tried to match her smile, "You're right, ok, I am all yours."

She seemed to like that response. She said, "You're a businessman and a capitalist, a powerful man."

"Guilty."

"Then I bet you would like to be around more powerful people." She continued.

"I don't follow."

She smiled again and asked, "Are you following the election?"

"Hard not to, the campaign ads and the news are full of it. The only other story that seems to run besides those are the terrorist attacks."

She nodded, "Do you think the attacks would have happened if President Adams had lost the election and Whittaker had been elected?"

He knew the factual answer but said, "I don't know. Do you think it's because she is weak on law and order or something like that?"

Her smile changed to sly, "Maybe."

"She doesn't seem weak on anything to me." Kostas, having been deployed at one time with the now sitting President in the Middle East, knew LeAntha was not weak on anything.

"Kostas, are you a Democrat or Republican?" she asked with a tilt of her head.

"That's an interesting line of questioning. I'm an Independent. I don't believe in the two-party system."

Their food arrived, and the server poured more wine. Kostas said to the server, "Thank you; it looks great."

As the server departed, he smiled and said, "I'll be right back. I'm going to run to the restroom, powder my nose."

She returned the smile and said, "What a handsome nose it is. I'll be waiting."

With that, Kostas stood and placed the napkin on the table over his cell phone, then walked to the men's room, leaving the decoy phone on the table. As Kostas entered the restroom, he dialed Jess's number from the fake restroom attendant's phone.

"Thanks Jim."

Jim nodded and started cleaning up the sink area.

256

Jess picked up on the first ring, "Please let me end this crap."

"Not yet, Jess. Jim says hi. What is she doing now?"

"Looking at your texts, obviously. Can I send one that says Marika sends her love?"

"Funny, Jess. Anything else?"

"Yes, the Mickey Finn is in your rice."

Referring to the term for a drug that is used to incapacitate someone by lacing their food or drink, sometimes also called a Mickey for short.

"Try to stay away from the center of the plate portion of the rice, and eat from the outside," she reported.

"Thanks, Jess, you're an incredible friend and guardian angel."

"I hope she gives me a reason, that's all I'm saying."

Kostas ended the call, gave the phone back to Jim, washed his hands, and thought to himself, "Thank the gods on Olympus; Jess was on overwatch."

When he got back to the table, he said, "Now, where were we?"

Still keeping the forced smile on her face, Hogan said, "We can talk all about that later, let's enjoy this wonderful meal and the rest of the wine. The fish is incredible."

Kostas smiled, picked up his fork, and placed a bit of halibut and rice into his mouth. "Hmm, you are right. The rice particularly pairs well with the wine."

From her overwatch position, Jess muttered, "godsdamn you Kostas."

Chapter 61

As they rode the elevator up, Hogan made sure her body was pressed up against Kostas's, hip to hip, and placed her arm around him, pressing her right breast into his torso, hoping that that would distract him.

She was assessing if he was armed; he knew.

He was. *That will at least keep her honest for a little while*, he thought to himself.

There was another couple in the elevator with them. Kostas recognized them as Allison and Chris, two MGSI employees that Jess had assigned to this part of the security detail.

Kostas was a little surprised to see how enthusiastic they were about their role in this; they couldn't keep their hands off each other. He made a mental note to review the company's fraternization policy when he got back to the office—if he got back alive.

Allison and Chris's role was to portray a young couple celebrating a milestone of some kind, or maybe even a passionate fling, while ensuring that Kostas remained safe while he and Hogan were out of Jess's view. Once they got into the room, Jess had it from there. Both were armed and good at their jobs, and Kostas felt as safe as he could at this point. Despite the young couple's appearance, both were combat veterans of Afghanistan and other operations around the world. Allison, a former Navy linguist and cryptologist, is similar to Jess's Army background. Chris, a seasoned former Navy SEAL.

The elevator car's bell chimed, the door opened, Allison and Chris stepped out of the elevator, and made room for an elderly woman to get onto the elevator, "Oh, my. I wanted to go down to the lobby, not up. Silly me." The doors closed.

Hogan looked a little annoyed, but Kostas smiled at the older woman and said, "No problem, ma'am. We only have one more floor to go, then you can ride it down."

Mona Fye stepped into the elevator car disguised as a woman at least ten to fifteen years older than her actual age. Mona officially retired from MGSI over two years ago, but she could never resist a small, manageable mission to stay sharp, in her words.

She jumped at Jess's request to play her part in the plan now that she had fully recovered from her hip surgery the year prior.

Mona smiled sweetly at the Kostas and Hogan, then said, "You are the cutest couple. You remind me of my husband Stan and I when we were young. How long have you been together?"

Kostas smiled a goofy grin and replied, "Seems like only yesterday we met." He gave Mona the predetermined code, indicating that everything was okay. If he had used the duress code and replied, "It seems like forever," then Mona's smile would have vanished as she pulled her Glock from under her shawl, which was covering both the weapon and her hands.

Mona was a seasoned operative; retirement did not slow her wit or her shooting skills, which she routinely demonstrated at the MGSI firing range, a retirement perk.

The elevator chimed again. "This is us, come on, honey."

As Kostas and Hogan exited the elevator, he uncharacteristically reached down and patted Hogan on her ass. He noticed that this unexpected and demeaning physical act in public had infuriated Hogan. However, she quickly calmed and regained her composure.

Nodding at Mona, and in a patronizing tone, he whispered in a slight slur, "Good night, ma'am. Don't forget to press the lobby button. Getting old takes its toll on the mind."

Kostas couldn't be sure, but out of the blurred corner of his eye, he thought he saw Mona flipping him the bird as they exited the elevator.

A moment later, after the elevator doors closed, Hogan confirmed his suspicion. "Did you see that?" she asked.

He laughed and said, "I shouldn't have said that last line to her."

Hogan played with the buttons on his shirt and cooed, "I like that mean side of you, maybe I can see it more."

By Jess's design, their room was only one door down from the elevator, allowing them to get back into her view quickly after exiting the elevator.

Kostas unlocked the door and allowed Hogan to enter first. According to Jess's plan, if Kostas entered first, the next person through the door, as well as any others, would be dropped to the floor, never get back up again.

Chapter 62

As Jess looked through the high-powered rifle scope, she sighed in relief. Everything was going to plan, so far.

She watched through the scope as Kostas walked into the bedroom and made a show of what seemed to be an overly dramatic yawn and a little unbalance in his step. She thought to herself, *don't oversell it Kostas.*

Jess scanned the rest of the room with the rifle scope. Hogan was in the bedroom doorway, a smile on her face.

Kostas continued to the bed, a bit clumsily, removing his suit jacket and shoulder-holstered gun and the one holstered behind his back.

Jess had told Kostas that to convince Hogan that nothing was afoot, he had to demonstrate normal behavior, like having his primary and backup weapon on him. At the right moment, when Jess was dialed in and providing cover for him, he would voluntarily disarm himself, allowing the opportunity for Hogan to reveal her true intentions. Kostas placed his weapons on a nearby credenza, then sat on the edge of the bed, slouching a little.

"So, I am listening." He said with a small slur.

"Why Kostas, are you drunk?" Hogan asked.

"Why? Are you going to take advantage of me?" he said with a stupid smile.

"Maybe."

"A guy can always hope," still with a silly and tipsy smile.

"I had hoped you would have come around earlier. We could have been on the same side, good versus bad."

Kostas, looking confused, said, "What? We are on the same side. Like you said, good versus bad."

"That's the thing, Kostas, you think you are on the side of good, you are not. You are on the enemy's side."

Again, looking confused, "What are you talking about?" He said as he lay back on the bed.

"Kostas, we could have been great together, but sadly you are a liability and to be completely honest, a royal pain in my ass. You have been fucking up plans that were years in the making all because you were on I-95 at the wrong time."

He managed to right himself on the bed slowly. "What?"

"Those currently in power are the enemies. Enemies to this country with their policies and inaction while in office."

Kostas, whose head was now looking down at his boots, heard metal clinking together, then the unmistakable sound of a suppressor being threaded to a gun. He slowly looked up as Hogan was indeed attaching the suppressor to a Sig 9mm pistol that she removed from her black matching purse, the same Sig model as Kurt Vista's pistol.

"So, kill me like you killed Andrew Kenna?"

"In short, yes. If you were more of an actual operator instead of an analyst, I wouldn't have gotten the drop on you like this."

He managed to slur, "I prefer the analyst role… besides I don't need to be an operator."

"From where I'm standing, that's where you're wrong, Kostas," then scoffed, "You're done. There's no way out of this for you. Analyst or operator doesn't make a difference. Your end is now. It's too bad, we could have had fun together."

Lifting his head up straight, he said, "That's where you're wrong, Agent Hogan."

Once again, he saw that quizzical head tilt look, which might have been three heads, but it was there nonetheless. "What do you mean?"

"Did roofie I slipped you messed you up to the point where you're delusional?" Then she laughed, obviously enjoying this.

Still looking at the now blurry three heads of Hogan, he said, "I don't have to be any of those things right now, all I need is Sparrow."

With her head still tilted and her eyes squinting to try to solve this riddle, she began to raise the gun, "What are you talking about, a sparrow?"

"No, not a sparrow," the room was spinning now, "but Jessica Sparrow."

As the words left his mouth in a slur, a single 7.62x52 mm hole surrounded by a network of splintering spider web appeared in the glass window of the hotel's bedroom, directly behind Hogan.

With his eyes now closed, Kostas heard the fracturing glass and a thud as if someone thumped a watermelon to see if it was ripe.

That thud was in concert with the moment the frontal lobe of Agent Hogan's brain exited from her skull in a spray of red hair mixed with white bone, pink tissue and bright red blood.

As Hogan's body collapsed to the floor, Kostas fell backward on the bed mumbling, "I had to sell it..."

Chapter 63

"Eagle Eye Command, this is Rover One!" came the Hendrick's voice through Jess's earwig. Still keeping her rifle trained on Hogan's now lifeless body, Jess responded with three clicks of her comm, signaling she was listening and to proceed with recovery and evac of Kostas.

"Jess, the kitchen security team tried to recover the tainted food from the plate for evidence, but the entire portion of rice was gone; it looks like it was consumed."

"Shit, Kostas," Jess muttered, thinking to herself, *you didn't have to sell it that hard.*

She then replied, "Hendricks, have the medics transport him for suspected poisoning. Inform them of our suspicions. Send two from our team with the ambulance to guard him until I arrive. I'll head to the hospital as soon as I can. Make sure they document whatever they find in his stomach and blood for the FBI."

"Copy that, WILCO," Hendricks responded, then clicked off the comm.

Chapter 64

Kostas woke in Richmond's St. Mary's Hospital with a harsh voice and a sore throat, largely due to the large bore orogastric tube that was inserted into his stomach to remove its contents.

When he tried to sit up, he winced as if he had done a hundred stomach crunches the day before, then was punched repeatedly by Mike Tyson, both sides of his abdomen were radiating pain.

A voice in the corner said, "Stay down."

Jess brought over a cup of water and a drinking straw. "Take it slow."

In a rough voice, he whispered, "Did they use any lube at all?"

Jess smiled and jokingly said, "No, I told them not to since you disobeyed me on the rice and the Micky. It's a little punishment for ignoring a direct order from the mission commander."

"I had to sell it." He whispered.

"That was a hell of a gamble, you fool. It might have been cyanide for all you knew and not just a Mickey Finn."

Taking a sip of water, he whispered, "Calculated risk. Poisoning me wasn't her style. She wanted to be up close and personal, to let me know she was superior."

"She wasn't. Well, at least not superior to me and my skills, maybe superior to yours." She joked, then added, "Still, it was one hell of a gamble."

He tried to laugh, but was only rewarded with a cough and pain. Kostas coughed again, then said, "I heard the glass splinter and the thud; that's all I remember."

"Hogan was raising the Sig. I already had her confession of events recorded and her admission to murdering Andrew Kenna. So, before the muzzle was on target, I pulled the trigger. The video and audio files are already in the hands of the FBI and DTRA."

He nodded several times in understanding, "Thank you, Jess. Marika?"

"Safe at the Hellenic Army Training Center in Litochoro, Greece. Still is pissed at you."

He nodded again, "Thank you, Jess, I can never repay you."

"I'll think of something." She winked and smiled. "Now, get some rest."

"No, get me home. Don't make me walk or call an Uber." He replied while slowly swinging his bare legs from the hospital bed to the floor. He stood and turned around looking for his clothes exposing the back of his hospital gown and his bare ass.

Jess remarked, "Marika is right."

"About?" Kostas asked.

"For a guy, you do have a nice ass."

Chapter 65

Kostas sat down in Wade's office, looking like he had aged another ten years in the last few days. "You look like shit," Wade said.

"Good, my look matches my disposition right now," Kostas said after taking a drink of water.

He continued, "With the evidence that Frank and MI6 put together for us, pretty much everything is contributed to Lawrence and Red's militia group and Hogan. Hogan seems to be the mastermind behind all of this."

"Seems so, truly unfortunate. I am still shocked to see a career FBI Agent's involvement in something that ran the gamut of a mass terrorist attack on two major interstates, the potential of a nuclear disaster, and a mass transit attack." Wade said, shaking his head sadly.

Kostas nodded his head, seeming to agree, then looked down at the floor. Then, he changed the direction in which he was moving his head to a distinctive back and forth motion, confused and disappointed.

Wade not registering the change in Kostas's manner said, "All for getting a political candidate in office? Seems just wrong here in the United States, what happened to democracy, free and fair elections, and the will of the people?"

Still shaking his head. Kostas simply asked, "Why?"

"Why what?" Wade asked with a look of puzzlement.

"Why did you do it, Wade?"

Now Wade was shaking his head back and forth, abandoning the look of puzzlement, then smirked, "God, this would have been a lot easier if you were still in uniform. Damn it, you just couldn't see it from OUR point of view, you just couldn't give Hogan a chance to explain why OUR solution is the best course of action for this country. All you had to do was listen, and I was certain you would see the right of it. I told her as much."

He paused, "Hell, Kostas, look at everyone that was in Program Paratiro, the KIAs, the deaths from cancer, and your own beryllium exposure and the scar tissue in your lungs. Bobby, Zielinski, Marten; all dead or suffering from cancer. Look how many others are dead and suffering with no accountability, no actions to protect us from those horrors again. None of this would be necessary if the right president were elected. We can fix that; we need someone strong as Commander-in-Chief. Can't you see we need someone to make things right, use the heavy guns when needed, not all this diplomacy kids glove bullshit."

"And Whittaker is that guy?" Kostas asked.

"The best chance we have. At least he listens to the like-minded people in the right political party and couldn't care less what the rest of the world says and is focused on the American people and the American people only."

"Or who he defines as an American. So, a dictator? And the legitimate American citizens' will, the will of the people, has no bearing on that?"

"Shit Kostas, you know as well as I do, 99 percent of so-called Americans don't know what it takes to preserve this Nation's security. You know that!"

"Wade, I'm not here to dispute your numbers, but I will say it's not my choice. It's not your choice, or any one political party's choice. It's the Country's choice. That is why our forefathers created the system that they did. What you are proposing is exactly what our forefathers fought against."

Kostas paused, "So it was you on the other end of the calls with Hogan, altering your voice with an app. You led everyone to believe it was Lawrence."

"Hell, Lawrence has been dead for weeks, he and Red both buried in one of Lawrence's concrete projects somewhere in West Virginia. Hogan took care of that herself. Neither of them are likely to be ever found; both brothers became liabilities just like Andy, I couldn't allow that."

"So, you started setting up your pins in front of me so I could knock them down for you. Tie up your loose ends, including Hogan?"

"You were always smart, too smart for your own good, Kostas. As far as Hogan, I knew eventually she would be under surveillance, I decided to put it to my advantage." Wade paused and looked at Kostas with a small grin. Then asked, "A point of professional curiosity, how did you get from her to me? I know she didn't spell everything out for you before Jess painted her brains all over the room at The Jefferson."

"For professional curiosity's sake, I'll allow it. It was something she said and something you didn't say."

Wade's grin went to a forced smile, and he said, "Go on."

"Before she could pull the trigger on me, she couldn't help gloating that she got the drop on me, and she seemed hell bent on demonstrating that she was somehow superior to me. She said, nice of you to clean up OUR loose ends. The way she said it was not like the typical Hitler salute that was recorded during surveillance." Kostas said in a mimicking tone, "God bless OUR Nation."

Then he paused and stared at Wade. He continued, "Her tone was more familiar, not a Hitler Youth response like on the recordings. It conveyed a tone of partnership, a team, *'our'* loose ends."

Wade squinted his eyes at Kostas.

"She also made a small slip of her tongue at Lemaire during dinner. She called you Wade, not General Morris."

"Then you either intentionally or unintentionally left out the fact that you visited Bobby also before his death, days before I did. That omission gnawed at me for days. You had previously told me at Bobby's funeral that you visited him at the hospital. I bet Agent Hogan was there at the hospital, too."

He paused again, "Then it occurred to me. I would be the only one on the team who would know that even happened since you weren't supposed to even know Hogan back then."

Kostas paused to let that last sentence hang in Wade Morris's mind, then continued, "There was no way for you to be sure of one thing—if I would even remember you told me that. Second, did you or did you not even tell me you were there? Did Bobby maybe tell me once I came to visit?"

He paused again for effect, "I'm sure you couldn't remember for certain. So, you rolled the dice and hoped it wouldn't come out in the investigation. When I added both your name and mine to my investigation board back at MSGI, I noticed things in a different light. I knew someone had to be covering for Hogan, feeding her detailed information; that person had to be you, Wade. You pretty much confirmed it when you explained the connection between Bobby and Hogan. I may or may not have found out all of that independently from Frank and MI6, but you decided to get ahead of it. Add to that, there was no way Hogan could have access to that level of detail on the MISPs scenarios from Bobby. He would have had to literally hand her the files on the I-95, North Anna, and the Tube scenarios. It had to be someone else providing that kind of detail. There was only one person with that level of knowledge that wasn't accounted for. It had to be you, Wade, by process of elimination of everyone else."

The General looked nervous. A single drop of sweat ran from his right temple to his mid-ear.

"General Morris," Kostas paused again, hoping the mention of his rank and name would send a message.

"What I don't understand, Sir, is why you should proceed with the other MISP scenarios. You made your point on the Virginia interstates. You undermined the current Administration in the Oval Office on behalf of Whittaker and his followers. Why continue to put thousands of people at risk?"

Wade continued his forced and frozen smile, then clasped his hands softly together, then slowly threw them into the air in a gesture of *What are you going to do?*

Then Wade Morris cleared his throat, "Once again, Jess had the right of it. Mad dogs. Unauthorized missions on Red's part. The dumb hick wanted to see the world burn. Especially so, after Hogan told him that Lawrence was in custody, when actually she killed him and disposed of his body, that's why Hogan had to also dispense with Red while he was here in Virginia. He had ordered the green light locally with his militia boys on North Anna and the VRE."

"So, the raid on Andy's house was all a setup to clean up that loose end?" Kostas asked.

Wade looked annoyed now, "Of course it was, the first loose end to be dealt with. The raid was well planned out for days between Hogan and me; that's why I slow-rolled you into the operation when I did. I knew you would want to be there and would likely mess up Hogan's and my objectives. I have to say, Andy was loyal and generous with his funding of our operations, but ended up just another liability after Rizzarreo's widow opened her mouth to you."

"So, you had her and her daughter killed?" Kostas asked.

"The daughter was unfortunate collateral damage, wasn't even Rizzarreo's own kid. You see, Kostas, that's the thing when you send people from a militia to do something, and not well-seasoned soldiers. The militia members usually don't come with too many scruples, just opinions. A lot of opinions. Andy was full of them also, so was the widow, but a handful of Red's guys got the job done on the singlewide."

"Wade, why did you even bring me in on the Joint Task Force in the first place? You could have let me ride the bench as a witness to what happened on the interstate only. You had to know that I would be a liability or at least a complication in your plans."

With a small sarcastic laugh Wade said with a shrug, "I had to make chicken salad out of chicken shit. Bringing you in wasn't my choice; it was out of my hands. Once the Director of the FBI and DTRA's Director briefed POTUS, they suspected the attack was a copycat of Program Paratiro. On top of that, add the fact that a former member of that program was a witness and the only resistance to the interstate attacks, she insisted on it. Those two fucktard directors let her know who you were and your company's pedigree. Shit! I bet LeAntha had forgotten everything about you up until that point."

Laughing again and shaking his head, he continued, "Didn't have much of a choice at that point, this current so-called Commander-in-Chief tied my hands. The best I could do is try to contain you. Hell, I should have known even that would not work with you for fucks sake." Wade was laughing again. "Gods damn fucking Alpha."

He composed himself then continued, "I must admit Kostas, the reaction from Hogan at the first briefing in the Dulles Room was genuine. She shit her pants when she realized who you were!"

He chuckled again. "Her outrage was sincere, having the killer of Rizzarreo standing behind my left shoulder."

"Then why keep feeding me information and giving me resources?"

"Like I said, chicken salad out of chicken shit. I saw the end coming after Red and his militia started to make moves on North Anna without authorization. It occurred to me that an opportunity to use you as a tool was sitting right in front of me, to tie up all the loose ends that could lead back to me, including Hogan. As you said, set the pins up and let you knock them down. I just couldn't manage to get rid of you. That was my mistake, I should have sent Kurt Vista directly after you instead of those two dumbasses from Michigan that couldn't follow orders. But you bested Kurt with a damn pocketknife. A fucking pocketknife!" he laughed again.

"Believe me when I say Marten was never supposed to get hurt, Marika either."

Kostas, with disdain, said, "I'm glad I didn't rely on you to protect Marika, I'm glad I put my trust and confidence in Jess."

"Yeah, you outmaneuvered Hogan and everyone else with that little Crazy Ivan move to evade our tracking of Marika. Hogan was livid. She wanted Marika for leverage, even a little retribution. I don't think I have ever seen her get as angry as she was with you. Red face matched her red hair every time she heard your name."

"I have a knack for that kind of effect on some people." Kostas quipped back, but maintaining his stoic look. "I knew Marika was in danger, and she would be used against me if they got their hands on her. Naturally, at that point, I couldn't rule you out as friend or foe. So, my faithful friends in Greece's 32nd Marine Brigade, along with an assist from MI6 and the Brit's SAS, were the only play I had to ensure her safety."

Wade's frozen smile melted away, then he asked, "Now, another question for you, Kostas. Why did MI6 care so much about what was going on in your own little version of a Baldacci novel here in the Colonies?"

"Simple, preservation of democracy and free and fair elections."

"Bullshit."

"A little bullshit, yes. You see, General, after I briefed President Adams, sorry I meant to say LeAntha, about my suspicions, well, MI6 was more than happy to lend a hand at her personal request, GWOT style. You see, the UK has violent extremist assholes like you wanting to take power and office also."

Wade's mouth went agape. "Dilbert, Vola, and President Adams? When?"

Kostas nodded and gave his thin shit eating grin to Morris, "Shortly after Jess's surveillance report got to me, she returned to Richmond the same night. Seven hours before you received it. My suspicions were enough to go up the chain. I couldn't rule you in or rule you out as a suspect, and as you keep pointing out, I am no longer in uniform. So, I went where I felt I needed to get the proper audience for my concerns and findings."

Wade looked dumbstruck. Kostas continued, "Another failure of Hogan's and your own intelligence apparatus. There is no way out of this for you, General."

"You never did follow the chain of command, Kostas."

276

Kostas shot back, agitated, "Again, not in uniform any longer, Wade. Besides having the ear of POTUS and the Directors of the FBI and DTRA would come in handy when it was time to take down Hogan. Jess was there to make sure it didn't turn bad, and it did, but you knew that, and Hogan paid for that with her life to cover up your involvement."

He paused, then added, "Wade, I always followed the chain of command, until the chain of command failed. Then I looked to mission success only," he said with a steely stare at Wade. "You killed innocent Americans, civilians that you swore to protect against enemies foreign and domestic."

Wade interrupted, "Always black and white with you, Kostas."

"No, Wade! Right and wrong. That's how it always is with me."

With a sad smile, Morris said, "That is what your problem always has been, ever since I've known you."

"What's that?" Kostas asked.

"You're too smart for your own damn good. You could have been a General as well, hell, maybe even a political candidate, maybe VP. But no, you always had to follow your own direction and not anyone else's. Could never get with the program, be a team player."

"Another point where you are wrong, Wade. I've always been a team player, and that has never changed. I am on the team of the American people, and that means they call the shots, not you, not Hogan, or those traitorous bastards that want Whittaker elected for the wrong reasons. That's why I joined the military, and that's why I left the military. I wanted to continue to do the right thing."

"The right thing, that's in the eye of the beholder. I've never liked that working-class hero bullshit chip on your shoulder Kostas. Couldn't follow your superiors, your betters. Just took shit into your own hands with no consideration for the bigger picture."

"Like you and Hogan did?" Then Kostas rose from his chair and said in a loud, projecting voice, "Corporal Williams, on me."

A moment later, Williams and Please assist the MPs in the hall with the arrest of General Morris."

Referring to the four uniformed Military Police waiting in the hallway.

Williams appeared in the doorway with several MPs, "It will be my pleasure, Alpha. Men this way."

As the four Army Military Police entered the office, they had their hands on their weapons.

Wade rose from his chair, took the US Army-issued M17 pistol from behind his back, raised it to his temple, and pulled the trigger.

Kostas pulled out his phone, hit the stop button on the recording app, and walked out into the hallway.

Epilogue

It was just after eight in the morning local time; one in the morning back in Virginia. Marika and Kostas were sitting in the river valley of Mount Olympus, enjoying morning coffees and listening to the sounds of the Enipeus River outside a small café that was among many other bars and restaurants along the riverfront.

"Do you want to go with me to Route 82 to watch the Arsenal match with Marten and Shane?"

Marika smiled, "I would love to, I'll let Jess and Tess know to meet us there once they get back from their hike with the kids."

A small television located above the café's counter caught Kostas's eye.

The scrolling news update at the bottom of the screen translated to: "The BBC World Service has confirmed that all the major American networks have called the US presidential election. In a record-setting turnout of voters in the US, the landslide victory is awarded to…"

Acknowledgments

To the men and women of our armed forces and allied services, your selfless contributions to Democracy and the lives of others go beyond words. Your courage and dedication have inspired much of this book. I salute you.

A heartfelt thank you to my wife, Marika, for putting up with me and all my— let's call them "quirks" over the years and for still loving me every day. Your support and love are the cornerstone of everything I do.

To our family and the people of Litochoro, Greece—your passion, warmth, and friendships have long inspired me, as well as the breathtaking scenery surrounding Olympus.

To Dawn, Doozie, Mona, and Lynne—your resilience and friendship over the years have been a wellspring of inspiration for many of my characters. Thank you for being part of my journey and my family. With a dash of Marika, all of you are Jessica Sparrow.

To 'JP'—thank you for your time, effort, and insightful feedback on the early drafts of the manuscript. Your tolerance of my sense of humor in and out of uniform over the years is an incredible testament to the person you are—never change. *By the way—does it take twice as long to read with one eye?*

To LeAntha—I would not be where I am today without your mentorship during my Department of Defense career. Your wisdom and leadership have left a lasting impact on both my professional and personal life.

To Shane—Your friendship over the last three decades as my wingman will never be forgotten.

To some of my favorite authors who have influenced me greatly over the years, without your writings, I may never have found a way to move forward in my PTSD journey. Thank you for your writings, your worlds, and your characters, which have inspired me to create my own. Organized in alphabetical order by last name:

Marcus Aurelius
David Baldacci
Bernard Cornwell
Nelson DeMille
Dean Koontz
Terry Mancour
Kurt Vonnegut

Finally, to my readers, thank you for coming along on this journey with me. Your support means more than you can imagine. I hope *No Longer in Uniform* entertains, inspires, and resonates with you. If this story encourages even one person to face their own challenges with courage, then it has served its purpose.

About the Author

Andoni Iapetus is an American author and a retired United States Air Force veteran, whose military career has profoundly shaped his writings. Drawing on his extensive experience in the Department of Defense, Andoni now channels his deep understanding of military strategy and human resilience into crafting compelling military thrillers. He is the CEO of a government contracting firm based in Virginia, where he applies the same strategic acumen that defined his service career.

When he's not navigating the complexities of the defense industry, Andoni finds solace with his wife Marika, splitting their time between the hustle of Virginia and the tranquility of a small village nestled at the foot of Mount Olympus in Greece. This dual existence, straddling two worlds, informs the rich, cross-cultural narratives that permeate his work.

Disclaimer

This is a work of fiction inspired by personal experiences, observations, and my wild imagination. Any inaccuracies of places, tactics, policies, or other elements of reality are either unintentional errors on my part or deliberate efforts to obscure actual events under my newly minted creative license as an author— a hallmark of all writers in the thriller genre.

Any resemblance to real events, people, or places is purely coincidental. This work is a product of my vivid imagination and should be regarded as such. Again, readers, it is a work of fiction.

Copyright © 2024 by Andoni Iapetus, LLC

All rights reserved. No part of this publication may be reproduced, distributed, or transmitted in any form or by any means, including photocopying, recording, or other electronic or mechanical methods, without the prior written permission of the author, except in the case of brief quotations embodied in critical reviews and certain other noncommercial uses permitted by copyright law.

No Longer in Uniform is protected under US and international copyright laws. For permissions, rights inquiries, or other information, please contact the author through official publishing or literary representation channels.

First Edition: 2024
Author: **Andoni Iapetus**

Made in the USA
Middletown, DE
10 September 2025